LOW TIDE

William Mayne

RED FOX

A Red Fox Book
Published by Random House Children's Books
20 Vauxhall Bridge Road, London SW1V 2SA

A division of Random House UK Ltd
London Melbourne Sydney Auckland
Johannesburg and agencies throughout the world

First published in 1992 by Jonathan Cape Ltd

Red Fox edition 1993

Printed and bound in Great Britain by
Cox & Wyman Ltd, Reading, Berkshire

ISBN 0 09 918311 0

For Lucy, Tom, and Jack Morris

1

It was one of those hot days in the town school-room. Miss MacDonald was explaining the map with the bald patch in the middle, where nobody had been. Charlie Snelling was teasing a spider on the school bookshelf, flicking little balls of chewed paper into its web so that it had to come out and look. Each time it carefully cut the wet paper ball out of the web, dropped it on the floor, and darned the web.

"What are we thinking about, Charlie?" Miss MacDonald was saying, several times, loudly.

"Oh Miss," said Charlie, without thinking at all, "spiders."

Everyone laughed. Miss MacDonald was quite pleased with him. "I suppose you are right," she said.

Charlie stayed baffled at getting something right. The spider went to the middle of the web and waited to see what happened.

"Yes," said Miss MacDonald. "You could say it was like a spider's web." She was pointing at the map still. The bald patch was Antarctica, and in the middle a lot of black lines crossed, going from edge to edge of the map, like the threads of the

1

spider's web. "Those are lines of longitude, and the ones like circles are lines of latitude."

"Please Miss," someone asked, "where's the spider, then?"

"I expect it's in the middle," said Miss MacDonald. "If it's in the middle, then where is it?"

No one in the school understood the question. They all had the sense not to say, "The middle". There was nothing in the middle of the white bald patch except black lines. That did not stop Miss MacDonald deciding that the class was going to find out.

"One of you might go there one day," she said. "No one has, yet, and we'd be proud of you if you did. We might be quite famous down here in Jade Bay."

They all knew they lived in Jade Bay. No one needed a map to tell them that. But Miss MacDonald told them all the same. However, it was a big disappointment, because there was no mark on the map for their own town. But she found Wellington for them, which was not even on the same island.

She went back to the white patch and told them it was the South Pole, and someone would get there some day, and they would hear about it. Not in this century, the nineteenth, she thought, but in the 1900s, which would be the twentieth century in a few years' time.

"It'll probably be Charlie Snelling," she said. "He's halfway there in his dreams already, and just be grown up then."

"There'll just be a big spider," said Charlie. "In a funny attitude."

When Miss MacDonald had done the places that

2

were or weren't on the map she went on with things no one could see. "In this modern day," she said, "we get told things as soon as they happen, all over the world. Now we have a telegraph office in town messages come from Auckland at any time of day or night. There is always somebody to listen, and always somebody to tap the messages out in code. That's how we get news of the world. That's how Charlie will tell us when he gets to the South Pole, if there's a telegraph office there. Then the whole world will know."

"Can we have a day off when I do it?" said Charlie.

"Every time," said Miss MacDonald. "But there are unknown places much closer to home. Think of the bottom of the sea. There are divers going down to the wreck of the *Alexander*, but most of us will never see what's down there, even if it's only as deep as the street is long."

There were some questions about the treasure in the *Alexander*, but Miss MacDonald did not know any more about that than the rest of the town. The divers were working from a Jade Bay boat, but nothing had come up yet, none of the gold, none of the silver, and not even a copper penny. All this treasure had been coming from England to Wellington.

"And just look out of the window at The Knuckle," said Miss MacDonald.

They all looked. They saw it every day, a big jagged set of mountains rising beyond the trees, and they thought they knew it.

"No one knows it," said Miss MacDonald. "It's quite unknown in there, and there's no map at all.

3

It's unexplored. We know the sea goes round it, and there are towns beyond, and I come from one of them so it's true. But no one goes into The Knuckle because it's too difficult. Also there is the Koroua, the old wild man of the mountains, unless he's a legend."

"We've all seen the smoke from his fire, Miss," said someone. Miss MacDonald would rather have the legend than proof of it, so she took no notice.

"When I've done the South Pole," said Charlie, "I'll do The Knuckle the next day. It'll be a knock-out for the Koroua. He won't eat me." The Koroua was supposed to eat people.

But Wiremu thought he should explore The Knuckle, because his people had lived here long before white men came to put a town at Jade Bay. "Hundreds of years," he said. "This is our land. Us and the Koroua. We call it *Ringaringa*."

"He's right," said Miss MacDonald. "Jade Bay has only been here fifty years next year, when we're going to have a celebration. Before that there was nothing here. They had to leave the first places they tried because of the floods, and start all over again. That was long before my time."

Charlie watched the spider, and chewed another corner from his book, ready to throw. Miss MacDonald told how the ship, called the *Albrecht Dürer*, bringing the supplies from the first settlement, had sunk on the way, and how the people had waited and waited for it to come, and then with heavy hearts realized that it had been lost, with its crew and their goods, without any trace.

"Maybe they met a war canoe," said Wiremu. "Eh?"

"The sea," said Miss MacDonald, getting on to shipwrecks, "is almost entirely unexplored."

Outside on the dusty street someone was walking in soft and sloppy shoes. Everyone knew who it was, in his slippers all day. They had already talked about him.

"Siggy," said Wiremu. Siggy sat all day in the telegraph office listening to the buzzer, and writing down the words that sizzled out of it. He sent messages back too, tapping them into the wire with his left hand, while he held his cup of tea in his right. Between messages he made boots, morse-coding the hobnails in like exciting news, row after row.

"Telegraph," said Charlie. "Who's got a telegraph message?"

"Never mind now," said Miss MacDonald. "We shall hear by the end of the day. We shouldn't be inquisitive, because it might be a family death, or something equally sad."

The shuffly footsteps came off the street and on to the school verandah, sounding louder on the wood, and then there was the quick and buzzy tap of Siggy's hand on the door, as if he were sending a code message ahead of himself.

"She's blushing up," said Wiremu. "You white people do, you pakehas."

"He keeps proposing," said Charlie. "My mother says. Marry me, my darling MacDonald."

"She keeps saying no," said Wiremu.

Siggy came in without being invited. He had a piece of yellow paper in his hand. The school stood up, politely. The spider did some running on the spot with all the legs on one side. Charlie thought

5

it was sending a message back to Siggy. Miss Mac-
Donald tightened her lips, put down the pointer
she had been using, and waited

"Yes, Mr Webber," she said, patiently. "What
can we do for you?"

"I thought you would like to hear first of all,"
said Siggy. "You will know more about such things
and you can tell your scholars."

"Indeed?" said Miss MacDonald. "Bring me the
paper, Charlie."

But Siggy wanted to bring it himself. He was
really soft on her, Charlie thought. Fancy him, and
fancy her!

Siggy handed over the paper, and then stood
and waited. He did not want to go back to his
telegraph office while he could stand and stare at
Miss MacDonald instead.

"Thank you," said Miss MacDonald, without
opening the paper, or even looking at it. It was
actual telegraph paper, but not a personal or private telegraph. They came in envelopes. "Thank
you, Mr Webber. I'm sure you are eager to return
to work."

"Well, there you are," said Siggy, and he turned
round to go back, looking disappointed. Miss Mac-
Donald looked at the paper, and when Siggy was
just going out of the door she said to him, "Thank
you, Mr Webber. This is very interesting."

But Siggy shuffled on his way, his fingers tapping out some slow sad poem on each other. The
door closed behind him.

"Sit down," said Miss MacDonald. "I told you
we heard things here as soon as they do in London
or New York, because we are as up-to-date as they

are. Today the rest of the world too is hearing about this. There has been a very big earthquake in the North Island. It sounds as if some people have been killed. The ground has moved, and the earthquakes are still going on."

She showed them the map of their own two islands, with little dots for towns hundreds of miles away, close to the earthquake. "There are Maori villages too," she said, "but most of them are not marked on the map."

"We know where they are," said Wiremu.

"Can we go and see?" asked a very little girl right at the front. Charlie thought it might be his sister Elisabeth, but it could have been her friend. "We might get some." She thought it was a sort of cake, not a quake.

"It's hundreds of miles away," said Miss Mac-Donald. "We can hear about it, and be very sorry, but we shan't see it or experience it. We have heard of it as soon as it happened, and I don't suppose many people know in London, because it is night time there."

She changed the subject, and did spelling until she rang the bell for the end of school. They said the prayer for the country and the school, one for the Queen, and another for the people in the earthquake towns. Wiremu had a private prayer for the Maoris.

They went out. People were talking about earthquakes, and thinking they were lucky not to have them often at all. In fact no one could remember one at Jade Bay. The only people who knew nothing about it were the divers, still coming back up the river in their boat after the day's work look-

7

ing for the treasure ship, *Alexander*. They were not from Jade Bay, but from Auckland or Australia, or further off still, like Norway or Japan.

"I've been in an earthquake there," said one of them, climbing up the river wall. "Japan. The houses are made of paper, they eat rice with knitting pins, and there isn't any good red meat in the whole country, so I'm not going to miss it. No, we haven't found the treasure yet, because we haven't found the ship yet. I tell you what, we want an earthquake to bring it to the surface, just push it up on a little island of its own so we can walk in and take what we've come for and go home rich. All that money is just there for the taking, but I don't think anyone has, because they wouldn't have found the ship either."

At home Charlie's mother said, "It's a sad day for the Mainland Maoris, but the ones that are left will soon start up again and go on doing nothing."

She thought the Maoris were too idle to do a day's work dusting and baking. "I'm sure I have enough to do to keep you two and your father clean and respectable," she said. "I haven't time for feasts all night and meetings all day."

But Charlie thought that feasts all night were the right thing to have, and meetings all day would be no worse than school. And the Maoris worked very hard at some things, like catching fish and wood carving. His mother did not know much about these activities, because women were not allowed to see wood carvings being made, or to go fishing unless they went alone. Also, Wiremu was his usual friend, and more fun than most pakeha, or white, boys.

8

"She doesn't mean it," he told Wiremu.

"But she is right," said Wiremu. "We want different things from life, and we stay alive to enjoy them. There is no difficulty."

"We'll go fishing in the morning," said Charlie. "You come and knock on my window if I'm not by the river, and we'll fish on the beach all day, because it is Saturday."

"And then it is Sunday," said Wiremu. They did not care for Sunday because it went on so long in church, with lessons worse than school days, far more people to watch, especially parents, and hard clothes with collars for boys, and dresses to the ground for girls.

"When I am grown," said Wiremu, "I shall fish all day on Sunday too. The fish are not in church, and do not mind which day they are caught."

"Don't wake my sister Elisabeth tomorrow," said Charlie.

"I shall be very quiet," said Wiremu. "But if she is awake then she will come with us."

"Come before she wakes," said Charlie. But no one knew when that was.

"Tea time," said his mother. "Goodnight, Wiremu."

Wiremu said, "Good night, Mrs Snelling," and went off home.

"I suppose he is a good boy," said Charlie's mother. "But how good is that?"

Charlie wondered what he thought. Pakehas liked the Maoris, even if they did not like work. But Maoris were better at hunting and fishing and all ball games.

2

In the morning Charlie was up before Elisabeth, but not before Papa had opened the store and sold tobacco to the divers. He got himself out of the room and closed the door. Elisabeth turned over, said something sleepy, and probably went back to her dreams.

The verandah creaked. The iron roof groaned a little. Out in the road the divers spoke to each other in their own diving language, which was ordinary English but full of words about optimum pressure and dive-time ratios.

Charlie had his line under the verandah, in the net. He had no rod, just a hand-frame with the cord round it, and the net was an old one. Charlie thought it had too many holes, some of them quite big, but Papa said it had too few. He said Charlie could buy some string and mend it, but he couldn't buy holes. He also said that you had to buy a complete hole, not half a one; and that string never came in half lengths because even when you cut it up each length was a whole one.

Charlie was not thinking about that. He was trying to get the net off the beam under the house without hitting the floor above and waking Elisabeth.

He went down towards the river so Wiremu could meet him at the landing stage. Today the divers were there, and he thought he could watch them getting ready and casting off.

The divers were not going anywhere at the moment. Their boat was still lying down below in the mud, because the tide had not come up to float it off.

"The later we start the longer it takes," said the chief diver. "The tide tables must be wrong out here in the wilderness, and not for the first time. But next week-end we're going across to Wellington to see a bit of life."

Charlie leaned on a mooring post and said he would like to go with them.

"No way," said one of the divers, and the third one told him to stop in Jade Bay and save his money.

"But nothing ever happens here," said Charlie.

"Too right," said the chief diver, and spat down into the mud beside the boat. "Not even the morning tide."

Wiremu came down the street with his fishing line and his spear. The spear had two points, and Charlie could never make it work because the fish moved away without twitching every time he stabbed at them.

Wiremu was pleased to see the river so low. "We can get out into some of those pools," he said. "I can use the spear. You can try again, Charlie."

"Let's get away," said Charlie. "Elisabeth could still come out and see us."

11

"If you see the tide give it a push," said a diver.

Charlie and Wiremu went up over the hill, because that was a quicker way to the sea than following the river down.

"It's far out," said Wiremu. "It is *hopua*, all pools and lagoons."

"We can come back up and cook what we catch," said Charlie. "We can have breakfast and dinner and tea, and get back at dark."

"Yeah," said Wiremu. "It's one of those days."

"And no Elisabeth," said Charlie. "We got away."

They climbed down the cliff on the other side and on to the sand at the foot. The sand went out and down, and became more and more sticky and dark. There were rocks standing in it, and pools round the rocks. At first there was nothing worth taking, but further out still, where the mud began, there were ponds with fish trapped in them. Quite big ones were swimming in shallow water, and occasionally jumping out.

"I'll have a go," said Charlie, climbing on a weedy rock to look all over one of the ponds.

But his go was only as good as it always was. Wiremu stood in the water and watched, without saying Charlie was managing badly. He took the spear when Charlie was about to catch his own bare foot. "I'll leave these little ones anyway," he said. "We'll go further out, eh? I've never been quite so far."

"I can't even hear the sea," said Charlie. "And where are all the gulls? I can hear one but I can't see it."

He went right round the rock, which was higher

than him, and chewed rough by the sea. He knew he had come right round because he came on his own footprints again, and the broader ones of Wiremu, who never wore shoes, even on a Sunday.

He was suddenly very vexed to see a third set of prints, smaller, and treading closer together than his own or Wiremu's. Then he knew what the gull had been calling: his own name; and that it was not a gull but Elisabeth, following him.

He followed her prints now. They led him round the rough rock. She had gone with Wiremu, and they were both looking at a smooth rock in the mud.

The smooth rock moved in the mud. It twitched and splashed. It opened its mouth and showed teeth. Charlie knew it was a shark, and that Elisabeth was too near it. He knew, all at once, that it could bite her in two just as easily on dry land as in the water. He ran across the mud to her, and pulled her away.

"Shark," he said. "that's a shark."

"It's a dolphin," said Wiremu. "They sometimes come ashore, but this one's stranded. I wish it wasn't so big, or we could take it ashore and eat it."

The dolphin slapped its tail and spoke a word. None of them knew what it said.

"You've got to go back," Charlie told Elisabeth. "They'll want you at home."

"No, that's you and Wiremu," said Elisabeth. "I can stay out. They didn't tell me not to. The divers told me you went fissing."

"But you haven't had your breakfast," said

Charlie. He could see that it was going to be difficult to get rid of her.

Wiremu was looking round for more dolphins, or anything else there was. "Look at this," he said. "Just look."

"It's a house," said Elisabeth. It was like a house. It was like a church. But it was a very big rock, like an island, standing nearly by itself, only some spikes of rock near it.

"We've discovered it," said Wiremu. "It is another land. It is an underwater mountain. The sea has never been out so far, and we are the only people who know about it."

They began to hurry towards it. For some reason it did not seem to get nearer, or to move away, only to get bigger as they went towards it.

That was partly because the ground was sloping downwards, and was lower at the rock. It was partly because the rock was a long way off. Charlie thought it was about a mile. He was ready to give up, but Wiremu said they must go out as far as they could, because this had never happened before.

Charlie floundered with him through mud and seaweed, where little fish were flapping in the air, things were making popping and bubbling noises, and other things were scuttling about, not getting out of the way but waving claws and very long feelers.

Nowhere at all could they hear the sea, which should have been close by and coming in.

"I want to go home," said Elisabeth, when a black lobster waved its legs at her. And she

14

screamed when a little squid took hold of her ankle in a friendly way.

At last they were at the foot of a cliff, where the remains of the sea still trickled in cracks. The cliff went up and up, and they were in its shadow.

"Reckon we should go back," said Wiremu.

It was Charlie who made them stay. He looked upwards. He began to see a way to the top. "It might be Wellington up there," he said. "We've come far enough out." But he forgot that, because he had no idea of what Wellington looked like, and because he had seen what was really on the rock. "But look," he said. "We have to go up. Look at it, just standing there."

There was a ship on top of the rock. He saw clearly the curve of its bow, the bowsprit pointing forwards; the cabin on deck; a mast hanging from its ropes, dangling down the cliff; there was the chimney of a stove, and tipped over the side there was an upside-down boat, into which no one had escaped.

"A ship," he said. "We found it, the *Alexander*."

"It just hit the rock," said Wiremu. "That sank it. We'll go up. It is no good. It is *pakore*." He meant "broken".

"We'll go home in it," said Elisabeth. "Sail, sail, sail." She looked round for it, not seeing what the others saw.

Wiremu led the way over sharp ground, up the scattery steps of the rock. Elisabeth came next, mostly on all fours. Charlie came last, to keep an eye on her.

They came to the top. Here the great fronds of

weed were lying thick as hair, soaking wet, clinging to legs, and with wriggling things still in them.

"Don't fall off the edge," said Wiremu, sitting
down in the weed. "It's a bad place."

They looked towards the land. It was a long way
off. The Knuckle looked lumpily back at them.
Nothing looked at them from the other direction.
The sea was still out of sight, and out of hearing.
The place where it should be was like land, with
hills and valleys, but no trees standing up.

"It's a new country," said Charlie. "We could
live in it. But look at the ship."

The ship was a sailing vessel. The mast was
snapped and over the side. Weed was growing
here and there, and water dripped from between
its planks. The parts that had been metal, like the
frames of the round windows, and parts of the
mast, were swollen with rust. The rudder was
smashed and cracked on the rock, and everything
was a blackish green.

"We found it," said Wiremu. "You did. It'll be
the *Alexander*. We can tell them where it is. They
don't need the tide."

They walked near the ship. In some ways it
seemed still to be sailing, perched on spikes of
rock. But the spikes held her fast.

"I can't read the name," said Charlie. "There's
an *A* and an *L*, for *Alexander*, but the rest has fallen
off."

There was an easy way into the boat, towards
the front where there was a little deck. They got
up, and stood on the nearly level planks. In the
sunlight they had begun to steam.

"We are the first people since it sank," said

Charlie. "The treasure belongs to us. But we'll never get to keep it."

"It'll be locked away," said Wiremu. "Pakehas lock everything up, just to be tidy."

There was a flag on a little mast, black and rotten and falling down when Charlie touched it.

Elisabeth found the ship's bell. It was hanging at the stern of the ship, near the drooping tiller. It was a big bell for a little ship, or a little boat for a big bell.

Then something was very strange, because no one touched that bell, but they began to hear a bell ringing all by itself, far away.

"It's the school bell," said Wiremu. "But it's Saturday."

Another bell began, and both rang together, firing and jangling. "It's the church bell," said Charlie. "But it is not Sunday."

Elisabeth put up a hand to the rope of the ship's bell. Charlie was looking at it to read the name, but he only got to A and L again. When Elisabeth tugged the rope the bell jerked, rang once, then dropped off its rope and went right through the bottom of the cockpit, splashing into water inside the ship. A smelly bubble came up.

Wiremu was looking out to where the sea should be. "Listen," he said. "I can hear something. What is it?"

"Just the sea," said Charlie. "They are ringing those bells a lot."

Into the still air of that morning there came a strangeness, a strong feeling that the air had grown thin, something like dizziness.

"We never got breakfast," said Charlie, to get rid of the hollow feeling.

"I think we ought to get off the boat," said Wiremu. "It might be one of those places we shouldn't go, Maori or pakeha. It feels like a *tapu* place to me, and we ought to get out of it."

"No, rubbish," said Charlie. "An old thing like this is bound to have pieces falling off it. If we just walk about carefully we'll be all right. Don't forget, there's treasure on here."

Wiremu looked seaward again. "I don't know where it's gone," he said. "I can hear it, but I can't see it."

"I can just see the cliffs near Wellington," said Charlie. "It's a long line right across, nearly straight." He looked back towards Jade Bay and The Knuckle, and the cliffs there. They were not a long dark line across the horizon. And only bells could be heard from their own land. From this other dark land there was a roaring noise, not loud, but coming closer, heard from far left to far right, like a boiling kettle.

"Don't sailors have chairs?" said Elisabeth. "I want to sit down."

"I don't know what's coming," said Wiremu. "I can't see it, but I know it's on its way." He looked from side to side, and shook his head, not understanding.

"We shouldn't be here," said Charlie. He wanted to blame Elisabeth, but knew that would not be fair. She had followed him, which was a nuisance; but he had led her here, so that was his fault. "We'll get into trouble."

He looked at Wiremu, hoping he knew what

18

would get them home now. Wiremu looked back, hoping the same thing about Charlie.

"I'm going into the room," said Elisabeth, looking into the cabin. "To play."

3

"It *must* be the other side of the strait," said Charlie, looking again towards the long dark line. "It's got clouds over it like land."

"That'll be it," said Wiremu. "We couldn't see it before because of the mist or something."

"It's just a new view, that's all," said Charlie, without believing it at all.

Elisabeth trod on a slippery piece of deck and sat down suddenly in seaweed with a splashing noise. She cried, but Charlie took no notice. He thought he could see waves in the distance, leaping and lapping at the foot of the cliffs, white foam dancing against rocks and climbing on ledges.

"The weather's getting clearer," he said.

"I don't know about that," said Wiremu. "What have I done wrong? Have I broken a *tapu*? Did I touch something I shouldn't touch, or go somewhere I shouldn't go? Why do I feel like this?"

Elisabeth tried some stronger crying, but by now it was only acting and did not sound real.

"You aren't hurt," said Charlie. "So stop it."

"I tell you what," said Wiremu, when he had looked again and again, "it's nothing. No one's been here before, so we're the first ones to find out how it looks."

"Yes, that's it," said Charlie. "It's a long way off as well, so let's look for what we've got here, because this is the *Alexander* and there's treasure in it."

"We'll get that," said Wiremu. "Then we'll catch a fish and eat it, and take the treasure home. The divers will be pleased if they don't have to work."

"They're not getting it," said Charlie. "We get it and we keep it. We'll be rich."

"No," said Wiremu. "You will be rich. I shall still be a Maori."

"But Elisabeth doesn't get any," said Charlie.

With everything settled they began to think about the treasure, about gold money, and silver money, and copper coins.

"I will buy everything in the store," said Wiremu, poking about in an open place on deck with the handle of the spear.

"Then my Papa won't have anything left," said Charlie. "He would not like that."

"Why are they ringing the bell?" asked Elisabeth. "It is going on and on."

"I do not know," said Charlie. "How can I know."

"But why are they?" asked Wiremu. "Is something happening. Is it all right here?"

Charlie looked round. Nothing had changed. To one side was their island with The Knuckle, and on the other the far away cliffs near Wellington.

Then from their own land there came a puff of smoke, and a moment afterwards a very loud

21

bang. There was another puff of smoke, followed by another bang.

"It is a maroon," said Charlie. "Two maroons. They are a signal for something we have to do. We have them in the store. They are made of gunpowder. They are fireworks."

"Do we have to go back?" asked Elisabeth. She was splashing about in the little cabin. She had stepped down into water. She hit her toe on a box in the middle. "There's no room," she said. "And it's ever so deep."

The water under the remains of the cabin roof was dark.

"It's in those boxes," said Charlie. "The treasure. I thought it was a table. But the table is on its side over there."

The table top had floated from its place and was upended to one side. Behind it were two places to sleep, and on the other side of the cabin two more. The top ones were empty. The lower ones were full of water. Wiremu reached in idly with the fish spear and stirred the one behind the table top.

"Something in there," he said. They all heard it rattle.

"No room," said Elisabeth, meaning the cabin was too small. "That big door." She meant the table top. Charlie went down into the water and lifted the top into its place. There were legs for it, rotting away.

Elisabeth came out after him and the water was still. But it began to shimmer and shake, twinkling at first, then becoming rough and dull with movement, and then splashing and jumping. Charlie felt the vibration in his ankles, then his knees, and at last in his teeth, if he held his jaws lightly apart.

"It is the boat," said Wiremu, holding out a hand that trembled all on its own.

Drops and spurts lifted from the water and landed on all three of them.

Elisabeth stepped away. "It is shaking the ship," she said lifting her feet, where she felt it most.

Wiremu looked round and knew something else was happening. "Everything is shaking," he said. "It is not just that water and the boat. Look."

The big rock the ship lay on was shuddering too. Long strands of seaweed hanging across it were all in motion, like switches of hair, but green, not blue-dark like Wiremu's or nearly white like Elisabeth's. Crabs and small animals were being shaken out, and fell down and down towards the ground, or bed of the sea.

The bed of the sea was ashake too. Pools in it were ruffled and broken like the water inside the ship. From some of them things larger than drops of water were jumping, fish escaping from the disturbance.

Further away, towards Wellington, stranger things than that were happening. The sea bed itself was shaking as if it were loose, and jets of mud were bursting upwards, exploding from the surface and falling back. Large rocks were rolling over, and heaps of sand were forming and falling and walking about.

Beyond that the cliffs were higher and nearer. At their foot the waves crashed wildly. In some places they rose like waterspouts, like huge

23

trees, falling in on themselves until nothing was left.

Charlie was alarmed at the way such solid things grew and then fell as he watched.

The shaking grew stronger. Charlie felt his arms moving on their own. Elisabeth sat down again, meaning to do so but doing it more quickly than she meant.

There was a groaning, breaking noise, and a spar on the mast moved on its own, swinging on its ropes, swaying outwards, and then arrowing in towards the ship. It hit the side once. Water fountained out of the cabin and knocked Charlie down.

The spar swung away and struck a second time. This time Wiremu was deluged, but he managed to stay upright.

The third time the spar swung away. A rope fastening it to the mast broke and fell away like a sea snake. The spar pointed itself at the ship and hit it in the same place for the third time.

It did not swing out again. It stayed in the hole it had made.

"I didn't like that," said Elisabeth. "It was cruel."

"It can't sink us," said Wiremu. "We're high and dry already. We're already shipwrecked before we came here."

He and Charlie went to the side and looked over. The hole was out of sight under the curve of the boat's side. From it water was gushing, making a waterfall down the rock. The water was dirty and smelt bad.

The shaking went on all round them. A wind

began to blow from the north, sudden and strong, lifting the new waterfall and flinging it aside.

The cabin began to empty. The spar had opened a way for the water to escape. As the water went down the tops of the boxes began to show, covered with slowly-settled silt, rounded and smooth, shiny with mud.

In one or two places the fishing spear, or Elisabeth's fingers, had marked the silt, spoiling the even flatness.

Elisabeth saw the thing first. "What is it?" she asked, because she did not like it.

Charlie looked and knew what it was. He did not like it either. He did not like it when it lay still. He liked it even less when it moved and smiled at him.

Lying in the sleeping place, where Wiremu had stirred the water, was a man's skeleton. Some of him was still in his clothes, leg bones sticking from the ends of his trousers, and a hand holding a hammer lying in the sleeve of its arm-bones.

The smiling piece had moved. The skull with its jaws in place rolled over once, and once again, then stepped down from the edge of the berth to a high box, then rolled to a lower one, and looked up at the sky through the cabin door.

Charlie expected it to say something. He stood up, but the wind knocked him flat again, coming so firmly now. Charlie lay where he had fallen, unable to get away, hardly able to get up.

Wiremu was lifting himself to look out from the ship. He saw the skull and did not want to look at it either. He made a face of sorrow and disgust, because he had disturbed the bones with his fishing spear.

"I knew there was something bad," he shouted. "That's why we are here, because that was what we were going to do. It is a bad thing." He raised his hand to point to the long dark line that they had thought was cliff.

It was not a cliff any more. It was a green hill, miles and miles long, sloping up from the bottom of the sea, and treading along it. As it trod it made the seabed shake. As it moved it roared. As it advanced it blew the great wind before it. In front of it the bed of the sea boiled and burst against its shore. It looked innocent and harmless in spite of its size, covered with grass, with here and there the white of lambs, or other creatures coursing their way up and down or from side to side.

Charlie longed to be in such a peaceful place, lying calm and friendly.

Wiremu pointed with the fish spear. Charlie looked, and did not understand what he saw.

On the hillside, as if it had been thrown away in a field, there was a dark thing. It was a ship, trying to sail and keep a course on a shifting flank of the great pasture. There were men in the ship, managing the sail, keeping a look-out, steering. One of them appeared to shout, but Charlie heard nothing at all. He began to understand that there was no hill, only a heap of water, as big as a country, coming back to its place.

The ship had a lot of sail up for this strong wind, and did not fill those sails. It seemed that the hill, coming along, was steady in itself, but pushed air ahead of itself.

"We shall sail too," Charlie shouted, but no one heard him. He knew they would sail, or be drowned, because the hill of water belonged here, and was returning here. At its foot the water was held back by the bed of the sea, and curved under itself. Roughness in the sea floor caused white water to be formed, and jets of foam to shoot ahead, and even up into the watery hill itself.

That seemed strange, because the water, sloping and leaning as it should never do, was more solid than it could be, seeming hard as iron.

But it was not so. The ship on it sailed along, tipped at an angle but acting as if it were upright, skimming that firm surface. But after it, and in the water, things were swimming as if no strange event were taking place. The fish were big, and in a little while Charlie knew them for whales, swimming high in the air behind their hill of water, diving and surfacing as if nothing had changed for them, seven or eight great bulls, and and a cow tending her little one. And they too went by, leaving Charlie guilty at not mothering little Elisabeth.

All at once the wind dropped, and they were in the weather of the hill, close to it. In a moment, Charlie thought, I shall step off with Elisabeth, and walk about on there, where the grass is deep.

The shaking stopped, and there was a beautiful calm that would last for ever. And the noise, which had been so loud, died away to a whisper from a friend.

In the glassy translucence something else appeared, waving its arms, looking out, wanting to catch something if it could. A giant octopus hung there like a portrait of the sun, all black rays, like a map of the South Pole.

All at once it was overhead, looking down with its huge eyes.

The wave carrying it began to fold round the ship on the rock, gathering to swallow.

4

Charlie felt the pushing coldness of the watery hill. It sparked drops at him and at Wiremu. Elisabeth clapped her hands at the octopus, at first in delight, and then to send it away. It rose higher and higher until it was almost overhead.

In its place, swimming with a smile because it knew what was next, was a shark, under the water, behind the water, a monster in a goldfish bowl with no glass, a monster looking out at its next meals, about to take them and eat them.

Elisabeth scrambled across the shaking deck and into the cabin. She went down out of sight into a place that felt better for her.

All the time the side of the hill pressed closer and closer. The noise came from the sea bed, where the water was torn and broken by rock and sand, set shaking by the weight of water coming along so fast. The hill itself was vast and silent, except when a wave went rippling up it in an impossible way.

Wiremu sat where he had collapsed, holding to the thick rust of a post, the jagged iron cutting into his hands. His mouth was open and he knew he was about to die without saying goodbye to his mother and father and brothers and sisters.

"The dog," he said, "will miss me. We put flowers round its neck on the Queen's birthday."

Charlie was thinking. He was working things out as fast as he could. He was thinking that someone should have told him about this new thing, a wave all by itself and as big as a hill, and that they were not to blame him for losing Elisabeth, that it was not his fault. No one could have known, he thought. He thought too that when anything is very strange indeed, like the low tide, then you go home and ask about it. He saw, all at once, what he might have known before, that if the school bell and the church bell are rung, and maroons fired, then you ought not to stay where you are.

"Liss," he called, "Liss," but there was no reply.

The noise grew too loud for voices to be heard. He could see Wiremu shouting, but he was the far side of a window of noise, and nothing came through.

Now the wave was curling right over them, and they were in the tube it made to left and right, and could see along it, green and dark, the noise of urgent waters pulsing, boom, boom, boom, like a hammer in the head.

Wiremu was still shouting. He seemed to have a difficulty in breathing, drawing in a chest full of air and then letting it out again. Charlie thought he meant something, but did not know what it was until Wiremu took a hand away from the post and held his nose, then made swimming signs.

"Take a deep breath," he was meaning, "before the water covers us."

However, there is a foot to a wave, as well as the forward-rushing crest and the tube that forms under and behind it. The foot of this wave was lifting itself up the sloping sea bed towards the land, being slowed down and becoming more turbulent. Now that part of the hill gathered itself and climbed the rock. It was from that part of it that most water came, surging up and over, and dousing Wiremu's new deep breath as he was taking it. He choked and spluttered. Elisabeth wailed, down in the cabin, and water came out of it, wild in the shaking of the earth, the rock, the ship.

There was a crash and a breaking, and the rowing boat that had hung over the side was torn away.

For a sudden moment there was calm. The ship shook no more, and the noise went away. The moment was soon over. The ship had been shaken from the rock. It was lifted on the slope at the foot of the wave, just as a football is lifted by the sloping instep of a kicking foot. Footballs then fly into the air, but the ship floated up the water gently.

The moment was not only over. It went quite away. This ship had once sunk with its cargo. Then it had the sea taken away from it on a low tide. Now the sea had come back and lifted it from the rock. Instead of overflowing it, pouring itself over the broken remains, the sea did something a little different. The ship rose up the water by itself, then went into the wave from underneath, up and up through it for a minute, no more, and then came out on top, on top of the hill.

Here it lay crooked on a treacly tide, lifting up and down slowly, the deck more or less level, and green water pouring away. There was a hush and a rest. Wiremu finished taking his breath and spluttered it out again. He let go of the post because nothing sudden was happening, or seemed about to happen.

Charlie had the corner of the cabin to hold, and had to lie down to do that. It filled with water again, and began to empty. Elisabeth sat rigid as the water rose round her and sank again. Charlie sat up. Down below the skull rocked and grinned, and the bones of its skeleton sat in a new order.

Inside the cabin Elisabeth was coughing. She was cross, and trying to say something, but kept having to spit out words half-chewed and unfinished.

Splashes of water were falling on Charlie. He saw them landing on Wiremu as well, coming down hard. They both put up their arms to keep the water from their eyes. The water was falling so hard that it seemed to bruise where it landed, making Charlie's eyes see black and dazzle.

It beat just as fiercely on his back, and when he drew a breath through his mouth it mixed itself with the water and he had to swallow it.

"It's rain," he said. "It isn't sea," because it had been sweet in his mouth. He let himself drink it. He thought of getting out of it too, and joining Elisabeth in the cabin.

He did not want to move. He felt hot, then cold, then that everything round him was going small. He wondered whether he was waking up from a dream. But he stayed uncomfortable and unhappy, and knew that he felt sick. It was not from drinking the rain, but from being on the ship. He was becoming seasick.

He would rather die. He let go of the corner of

the cabin, which he had been holding with one hand, and took the other from his head, where it had been sheltering his face. He curled up and lay on his side and thought he would cry.

Wiremu had stood up. The deck was heaving about under him, but he balanced on its movement. He look cheerful now, taking no notice of the rain. "I've got seasickness," he said. "Any minute now."

Charlie could say nothing. A horrible dizziness came on him, and he did not care about anything.

Wiremu was kicking him, not hard, but enough to wake him up. Charlie found he was cross about that and would get up and kick Wiremu for not caring.

He got up to do that. Sick later, he decided, kick first.

Wiremu was looking out at the sea, at the hill top of water they were on. "Got to see where we are," he shouted.

Charlie looked. There was water all round, because this was the middle of the sea. But to one side, if he looked downwards, there was not water. There was land. He and Wiremu, the ship and Elisabeth, were flying over land, fast and easy, higher than the trees, higher than houses, because there was one below, and then they had passed it.

They were not higher than mountains. Under a great cap of raining cloud sat The Knuckle, knotted and rugged, and coming towards them very fast.

Charlie thought it would be ridiculous to be shipwrecked up a mountain, because water does not go there.

This water was going there, and doing it very

fast. The brownish black rocks of The Knuckle approached faster than anything he knew, leaping towards the ship. Or the ship was leaping towards The Knuckle, running down towards it perhaps, because the crags were getting higher and higher.

One went by with a big bird rising and circling to escape, dropping away behind them. There was a wall of rock on the right, and then a slope to the left. Mountain ridges ran level on either side, and were coming closer.

The ship was going up a valley on its wave. On either side trees were being lifted from the earth and turned over and over, soil falling from their roots, so that they looked much the same either way up. They were then torn into two parts and crushed against rock. Their tattered leaves stained the water.

There was nasty pitching movement to the ship now, and noise began to return. Charlie felt ill again, and down in the cabin Elisabeth was already ill and crying for Mama.

Now the ship was rising as the waters rose on either side and began to spill over the ridges like waterfalls. Ahead there was the top end of the valley, where the mountain stopped it off. Water swirled ahead and met the wall of pure rock, where nothing grew.

The water turned round and came back, full of rubbish from the valley sides. The onrushing water carrying the ship rode over it, was lifted and lifted, but could not possibly avoid hitting.

Charlie knew it would break up, because it was only made of trees, after all. It would hit the mountain, and their journey on it would have been useless if it only led to Elisabeth being lost for ever, to Wiremu being drowned, and to Charlie himself being blamed.

He thought of that in bits. He and Wiremu were now much too busy holding on. The waters were in so much turmoil now that the ship rode like a horse that has never been ridden, bucking and jerking, leaping and jinking, turning in its own length, diving deep into water, rising high from it.

A few seconds away the head of the valley closed them in.

The ship struck. There was a crushing thud, and Charlie bit his tongue. Wiremu sat down. They both thought they were broken. The water came over one side and out at the other. The ship rolled with it, rolled back, took another turn at hitting the mountain, spun right round about three times in a whirlpool, and struck again.

Pieces fell off. Trees came alongside and pulled them away. There was a noise like a barrel rolling on a verandah, shaking everything.

The ship did not stop moving. It was suddenly tipped over one way, towards the front Charlie thought, and began to rush faster through trees, knocking them down on one side, then on the other. Something ran with it, and Charlie was not sure what it was, underfoot and enormous, carrying the ship along.

Trees hurried on either side. It was like being out in the forest, the leaves being bruised and smelling of sap.

Branches overhead reached out to strike Charlie and Wiremu, slapping on the deck, on the deck-house, and whipping at the stump of the mast.

Still under them ran water, strong and fast, carrying them through the countryside. They were no longer at sea but inland, somewhere in The Knuckle. Charlie raised his head and began to see mountains far ahead and high up, mountains that were not moving, and were unknown to him.

A branch knocked him down and he stayed down, because the blow hurt him. The trees stopped touching the boat, but still something bore it along.

"We'll go down and get out to the sea again," said Wiremu. "You wait."

Charlie waited, because there was nothing else to do. He wondered if going on a train was something like this travelling. He had never seen a train except in a book. Miss MacDonald had once tried to describe it, but she had been interested in the taps and basins in it, not in the engine she had not looked at, or the working parts she did not understand.

The ship touched ground again. It hesitated, lifted, and then was almost not moving, almost in silence. Some distance away water was tumbling and gurgling, splashing a long way down on to rocks. But the ship was not in water. It was floating in air, moving downwards on its own.

It was in water again before Charlie could experience enough of the floating to remember it well. He would have had difficulty in any case, because the ship had fallen perhaps forty feet before coming to rest. There was a blow, and a splash, and very cold water poured in over him, turning everything dark. Or perhaps where they were had turned everything dark.

The ship was in a deep and narrow place of rock, held in a fast cold current, and moving along only feet from the sides. Not far away, but further off all the time, a waterfall was making harsh noises, as if it had gone wrong.

Wiremu was lying unconscious on the foredeck. Elisabeth had been thrown into the cockpit and lay not moving, her hair pulled forward and showing golden at the back of her neck, which was pale as a doll, almost having the same stitches to attach the hair. Charlie himself sat against the stump of the mast.

The boat moved slowly but jerkily, catching on the sides of the gorge, rubbing on shoals, pivoting on rock, and gradually the way grew wider, opening into something like a lake.

The ship drifted down the water. Sunlight came in for a time, and then was hidden by the mountains. There were dead fish floating on the water.

Elisabeth and Wiremu did not move. Charlie wanted to see whether they were breathing. He could move his hands, but his arms were weakly useless. His legs, spread out in front of him, were entirely useless. He could not move them. They were not uncomfortable, because they felt nothing. Only his back, against the wet wood, throbbed and ached, and set him longing for water and Mama and comfort.

A long time later the water was black, the mountains grey, and the sky was night. The ship drifted on.

5

It was dark for a long time. The moon came up into the sky, slowly, slowly, ugly like some horrible lamp, and Charlie hated it. It was worse than the sun. It was unshaded, glaring, and cold. It moved so slowly that it appeared not to, and yet fast enough to be crossing from the mountains one side to the mountains of the other, miles and miles of sky.

Charlie could not move. His head would sometimes stay up, aching. He could not lean back at all because some thick ring on the mast forced his neck forward. Whichever side he put it to the other side ached. Now and then it fell forward on its own and he began to choke on a dry throat. The dry throat would not clear itself because he could not cough. He could not even draw a long breath because of the pain in his spine.

The boat was lying level, and seemed not to move. But something made it sway from side to side, heave backwards and forwards, and have fits of trembling and wavering, as if the water had become lumpy.

As well as those movements, which belonged to the ship, it was turning slowly on the water, facing

38

a different way moment by moment, showing what was round it.

Charlie expected to see the open sea reaching towards him somewhere, an inlet between mountains. There was nothing like that; the edges of the water were the same everywhere, tree shadows at the edge, trees rising beyond, and then a roof of dry rock. On one or two of the high sloping slabs snow was lying.

The moon that let him see around also helped him to know which way he was looking. It stayed nearly in the same place a long time, and he came back to find it touching his face. He was sure, after a time, that the coldness of the light was reflected from the high snows.

The ship began to creak against itself. The dark wood, wet with shipwreck, began to change from black. It started to be covered with white. Charlie thought about salt coming out of the timbers until he felt frost tightening round him, starching his shirt collar stiff against his neck, pulling at his hair, freezing it to the mast so that it tugged and snapped when he moved his head. There were dazzling points on all the parts of the ship he could see, tiny button rainbows like spider webs made by ice spiders.

The frost painted itself in harder and made the deck and cabin top brittle with ice. He saw it wrap Elisabeth and Wiremu, tying them down so that they were part of the ship, part of the night.

He spoke their names, but they did not reply. He spoke his own name, because no one else did, but it was like being haunted, and he did not try again.

39

There were waves breaking at the edge of the water, giving a distant sizzling sound like eggs being fried for ever. The waves were fixed, somehow, as if this part of the sea had no tides. There were surges, with the waves of one place higher at some times than at another. Charlie felt the reflux through the water each time, and related it to what he heard, like seeing the puff of smoke from the maroons before hearing the slow sound.

No one came. At last Charlie thought of giving a shout, but did not dare do so. For one thing, he knew perfectly well that Papa and Mama were not near enough to help, and for another, he did not want to call anything he would rather not see. He thought of the Koroua in the mountains, and did not want to see it.

For most of the time Wiremu lay where he was. But once when Charlie woke choking and had perhaps been asleep, Wiremu had moved himself, and was lying more on his side. Charlie thought he might be shivering, but it was hard to tell, because he was shivering himself.

Elisabeth did not move at all. He looked at her and looked, and knew she was dead. Then she snorted, or snored, or made some living sound, said something cross, and pulled one arm away from the coaming round the cockpit.

The moon rested on a spire of rock. Charlie waited for it to come in front of the spire, but it went behind, its light diminishing gradually, until it was beyond the mountains. It still shone on higher ground, still reflected the cold from the snow. The stars took over the sky. They were faint indeed on the frost, and perhaps were a part of it themselves.

Charlie found he was swallowing salt water. The salt water was from his own tears, and it dried on his face. He managed to lift his hand to his face, and it felt clumsy, like another person's. His face was being felt by a stranger, and his hand felt another stranger in his face, because some of the feeling had been frozen away.

He thought about other people. It seemed impossible for Mama and Papa to come here and find him and Elisabeth. It seemed quite possible for something else to come, for the Koroua to come out of his mountain and find all three of them.

Everyone knew that the Maoris had eaten their enemies, and still did so. It turned their teeth black, Wiremu said. His grandfather had eaten a pakeha man and his white lady, and his teeth were the blackest in the pa, the village where they lived. The Koroua ate nothing else.

Charlie would not have eaten anybody, because there was no one he liked enough. Eating others did not seem wrong to him, unless he was going to be eaten. Then it ought to be stopped.

So it was best now to be quiet and not be noticed by the Koroua. It was best to let the ship take them out to sea again, where the Koroua did not live. Sharks did, but they did not come aboard ships; you were safe staying out of the water.

The ship still moved. Wiremu was groaning on the deck. Charlie thought he heard him move and the big knife scrape on the deck. He could not see very well.

The darkness grew darker. Something began to

come between the sky and the stars. Black patches ate at them, but they would reappear. There was a scratching sound, and a rumbling down deep in the ship.

It stopped moving. The sky was blotched with blackness, but the blotches did not move. The stars shone through holes, which perhaps was all they did anyway. But now there was something nearer, something overhead, the same colour as the space between stars, but lying in front of some of them.

The ship stayed where it was. The waves that had crowded on to the shore now beat against it, heaving at one side and jumping up it, perhaps to look over, perhaps to get on board. There was more salty water on Charlie's face.

He went to sleep. He felt it coming over him, and knew his head was hanging and would be uncomfortable, but he could not keep himself awake. It was a relief to feel his pain going, to hear nothing, and to see nothing, and to find dreams coming along to tell themselves.

He woke up with a great start before he got right off to sleep, because the first dream was full of Korouas dancing and taking Elisabeth and Elisabeth and Elisabeth, each Koroua taking one, and biting pieces off, like a boy with a gingerbread man.

The second time that dream did not come, and Charlie was at peace. He dreamt he was at home, and that he was at the table waiting for his dinner, Mama at the stove cooking, Papa coming in and sitting himself down. It was a lovely dream, and it ended when Mama put a dish on the table and Charlie's plate was full at once. He was trying to find something to eat among all the hair when everything went wrong, because it was Elisabeth's hair, bright as fire, and he was waking and choking and seeing what was on the ship.

Daylight was on it, and speckly shadows. The black things were still overhead, the leaves and boughs of trees at the water's edge, where the ship now rested. The waves still lapped noisily against it and sucked at the rocky shore at either end. Sunlight shone on high peaks, but only a smaller morning light reached down to where Charlie was.

He tried to move, but he still could not. His back hurt and his legs did nothing at all, as if they belonged to two other people. He wondered whether they hadn't actually come off, and were lying there because they could not walk without him, and were sorry about it.

Wiremu was not there. He had moved, or been taken away, or fallen overboard, or the skull in the cabin had eaten him. Charlie did not know, but he knew he was not thinking clearly, surrounded by dream or nightmare.

Elisabeth was still there, with something different about her. At first he thought a snake was holding her, and then he saw that there was nothing to worry about. She was partly covered now with something nearly cloth, made from the broad leaves of flax stitched together. It was a sort of cloak that Maoris wore. Charlie did not remember Wiremu bringing it with him; but perhaps Elisabeth had.

What a strange game, he thought. Then he remembered why they were on this ship, where it had been, and what he had dreaded all night long.

"Wiremu," he said, croakily. "Elisabeth." The sound was like dry dust under the house, tasting of rats.

He saw marks in the remains of frost. He worked out where Wiremu had come to Elisabeth, and then gone to the edge of the ship and on to the land. He will be back soon, he thought. We shall be able to get home. I wish Elisabeth would wake up.

He knew she would, because she was not allowed to die. He told himself that several times, and then his thoughts slid away to Wiremu and what he was doing.

He heard Wiremu among the trees, very close, walking slowly. He waited for him, and was going to be glad to see him.

A branch with its leaves on was being propped against the side of the ship. Another long, dead, one came up beside it. They were shaken into being steady. Then something began to happen that Charlie could not recognize. There was only a small noise, and a little creaking. The two branches began to move a little, at first separately and then together. Then they were moved together, and replaced against the side of the ship again.

He is making a ladder, thought Charlie. He has tied the pieces together. I shall be able to walk down.

His legs, however, had forgotten how to move. He was sure that they would remember very soon, that they had gone to sleep for longer than usual, and would wake as soon as he stood up.

He smelt smoke. It had been coming from the stove in his dream, where Mama had cooked. He

44

did not want to remember what she had cooked, though the hair had been his share. The smoke made his nose twitch, and he was ready to sneeze. But the sneeze went away when the next thing happened.

Someone climbed up the branches and into the ship, hands first, then head, then body, and jumping to the deck.

Charlie wondered what Wiremu was carrying to make his hair look white and his hands strange. After a moment of that he saw with horror that it was not Wiremu, that the hands were another person's, and the hair was white with age, and long, long, long. So was the beard, tangled on the visitor's chest.

It was the Koroua, ancient and hairy, glittering eyes looking about him. He wore only a fringe of flax leaves, like the cloak that covered Elisabeth. He carried the long knife that belonged to Wiremu, and he walked crookedly with bent and shortened legs.

He came to Elisabeth, the knife in his hand, ready to slice her. Wiremu's knife would do that with its edge that was gleamed with a stone every day.

"Stop it," said Charlie. It was all he could say. A Koroua did not know how to speak, Wiremu said.

This one did not. It waved the knife with one hand, began to pick up Elisabeth with the other. It looked at Charlie, its blue eyes steady and dreadful as the moon.

"Oauigh," it said, showing its teeth in the middle of its beard. It took no other notice.

45

The long knife went down from its hand and thrust itself into the deck an inch or two from Elisabeth's face. Charlie was sure the Koroua had killed her. But the Koroua had not yet done that. With the knife standing in the deck it had two hands to gather her up, and it did so, clasping her close, her head lolling back, and her hair dangling. The Koroua held her with one arm, and took up the knife with the other.

It turned towards Charlie and grunted again, not once but twice, as if it had forgotten about words.

It limped sidelong across the deck on its bare feet, felt for the two branches, and went over the side as if it went down steps.

Charlie's heart beat and beat, and he thought it burst and turned the world black.

It was bright again in a little while, when the Koroua came for him. It stood beside him, then squatted. It laid the knife down. The knife had the dark stains of blood on it. The Koroua took hold of Charlie's head.

"Oauigh," it said. Its teeth were black from eating people.

6

The Koroua took Charlie's head in its claws. Charlie felt his own neck holding the head too, tipped forward, not wanting to see what was to happen, ready to hold for ever and never let go. But if the Koroua pulled and pulled then the head would come off. What else would the Koroua be wanting to do?

The Koroua turned Charlie's head upwards and turned it a little to the right and a little to the left. The claws were soft and warm, just like Mama's when she sat on his bed if he was ill, and wanted to offer a small hug.

Charlie remembered that and felt miserable all over, in his heart and in his head, too miserable to resist the Koroua. The Koroua looked into his eyes. Then it ran its claws down his cheek. It was strange for them to feel just like fingers, or perhaps it was all the more horrible. Wiremu and the other Maoris talked about the Koroua as if it were a sort of man, but it must be a sort of animal, because there is only one sort of man.

So he felt claws on him, not fingers.

The Koroua let go and shuffled backwards a little way on its strange legs, still looking at him. It was a blue-eyed animal, and the eyes were uncomfortably like a man's eyes, with white all round the blue part. Frightened dogs are like that, and the wildest of forest monsters must be too.

It put out an arm and felt the collar of Charlie's shirt. One claw was like a thumb, others like fingers. It let go of the collar and held its paw out. It looked as if it could shake hands if it wanted to, but of course it could not know of such things.

All the same, it looked at the paw and thought about it, and seemed to remember. It frowned. It had a forehead just like a man, but the rest of the head and face was lost in a huge bundle of hair, mostly white, with a few dark streaks.

It remembered what to do. It reached forward again, lifted Charlie's right hand from his left shoulder, where it had gone to keep him safe, and held it in a handshake, shook it in a handshake, and let go as handshakers do. It said something quietly, repeated it two or three times, then shook its head, and looked puzzled again.

Somewhere there was another voice. It was Elisabeth's, from outside the ship, from some place on land. She called in a small voice for Mama, but all the forest round her soaked up the words and there was no reply.

Charlie knew he must go to her. He began to push at the deck with his hands, but could not lift himself. There was a sharp pain in his back, and his legs were still without feeling and could not move.

The Koroua turned its back on him and looked over the side of the ship. Elisabeth gave a little shriek and stopped calling for Mama. Charlie tried to call out with his dry throat, and tried again, and a third time before his voice worked.

"Liss," he called, and his voice was wooden. "I am coming."

Like a nightmare, the Koroua tried to repeat his words in a lost voice of its own, somehow getting it wrong, imitating not only the words but the way they sounded when Charlie said them. It was a monster that could not speak, only talk like a parrot. It was the echo that came out from among the big trees in certain places, or from long walls or tall cliffs.

The Koroua seemed pleased with itself, saying things quietly in its throat, practising. It saw what Charlie was trying to do and put out its paw again. Charlie took no notice, because he knew it could not understand. It shook its paw, then took Charlie's hand again. This time it was not a handshake put a helping hand, or paw. It began to pull him up.

The pain was dreadful, like being sawn in two, starting at the back about the level of the belly button. The pain circled right round him all at once, and joined at the front. Charlie had to look to see whether a long spike had not been put through the belly button, nailing him to the mast. He wanted to say something about it, by way of a scream, but all his breath went away before he could use it.

The Koroua pulled him upright. It was terribly strong. And then Charlie was standing on useless legs, and the Koroua had him by the waist, so that he did not fall down again.

It thinks I walk on two legs like it, thought Char-

49

lie. But I am a man and it is not. How can it know? But we are both wrong, because I cannot walk at all.

His legs felt very strange. He could tell his weight was on them, because they felt it. They felt all sorts of things, like pins and needles all over, or quite cold and asleep in places; and in other parts of them there was an angry twitching and shaking that he could almost hear. They did not feel like reliable feet.

His feet looked strange, but without feeling they did not know how they looked. One was treading on the other, and the toes were cold. He tried to move them but nothing happened. You move your legs without thinking. They do it if you want, and you do not know why or how, but it always happens. It did not happen now. Instead there began a pain in the bones, throbbing and aching and, pounding and beating, and faintness in the head.

His legs began to turn red. He saw them doing it, and knew his blood was racing back to its place. Then everything thickened and became misty, and he knew that he was folding over in a faint, held round the middle by the Koroua. It has poisoned me, he thought. It bit me with black teeth. It will eat us all.

He knew, in the blackness that followed, that the Koroua picked him up and carried him, just as it had carried Elisabeth, over the side of the ship and down the boughs it had leaned against the side.

Later on he sneezed and his eyes ran. He woke up and opened them. There was smoke. There had been smoke before, but this smoke was cooking smoke. Someone was cooking fish.

He sat up. It was not easy. He stood up. That was very hard, but he did it at last, in spite of feeling faint again at least three times. His legs held him, but he held the trunk of a tree and looked round.

He was on land again. The ship was close by, perched on a bouldery beach, with water moving about under it and breaking with puzzled waves on a little beach. Trees began at once, and he held one (and it held him). The place was magically pretty among the little trees, with a small creek or stream running among the roots and bubbling across the beach into the water. The distant places among and under the trees were full of a dusky light, open and friendly but not very bright; birds sang and flew, and in the water beyond the ship a fish jumped and fell in again. Only the black side of the ship itself was a little ugly and black.

Not far off among the trees there was a fire, and someone was talking. He knew the voice was Wiremu's, not saying much, perhaps talking to himself. Wiremu laughed a little, pleased at something.

Charlie felt a disappointment. It was clear that Wiremu had overcome the Koroua all by himself and was now cooking their breakfast. Charlie had been able to do nothing, like a fat useless pakeha, and had left all the work to a Maori. That was all right for some people, but Charlie liked the Maoris better than he liked most pakehas, because there was more fun, a lot of plain talk about things Mama never mentioned, and plenty to eat – sometimes a meal would last a whole day and far into the night until everything had been eaten. He felt ashamed at not helping, at letting Wiremu deal with the monster.

In a moment he knew he had been right about Wiremu and the Koroua, because there was the Koroua's head, all complete in its huge bundle of white hair, lying between two trees, like a huge round cushion.

There was ferny undergrowth here too. He thought the rest of the Koroua's body would be under those fronds. But laid out on the springy leaves were other things that made him alarmed. There were Liss's clothes, from the brown Irish linen dress to the knitted stockings, everything, even the little shoes hanging on twigs.

It has eaten her first, he thought. Before Wiremu could do anything it ate Liss. But he was not sure, because something was being cooked now. He had thought it was fish, because he knew the smell of that. He had thought of fish with a stick through their heads, hanging in the smoke, to be hot and delicious. He thought of Elisabeth strung up in the same way, and knew it was his fault and that he should have taken her home.

He looked back at the place where he had been lying, a sort of mattress that made a bed of boughs and leaves. He thought it was probably a fire ready laid to cook him. The thought jostled around with those he already had.

He walked to the next tree. He wanted most of all to run away, but walking was the best he could do, and even then he had to hold something. He would run away if the Koroua was eating Elisabeth. But the Koroua was dead, because its head was there, beyond the next tree, between him and smoke on the faint current of air.

He stood by the next tree and let his legs rest by not moving. They were just as tired by that as by standing still. He started again, and found he could not reach the third tree without letting go of the second. He swayed for a moment, took a pace without falling, and another, and then held his weight on the tree.

He set out for the next one without working out how far away it was. He went past Elisabeth's dress, and her little buttoned bodice, the vest from underneath that, and two dripping wet stockings. Anywhere else, he thought, you'd think they had been washed if it wasn't for man- and girl-eating monsters.

The bundle of hair was next. It really could not be anything but the hair from the head of the Koroua. He did not like to touch it, but he had to make sure.

He took a piece of dead branch, quietly, so that the Koroua's head did not hear him, and rolled the bundle over away from him.

It sagged rather than rolled, and tufts of hair came off it. Charlie began to feel sick at the thought of the head inside, with its black teeth, the hair coming off it like pig bristles in the lard, when Mama made that in the outhouse.

He had to roll the bundle towards himself. He wished he was ready to run as soon as he saw an eye looking back, a tooth showing, the wrinkled forehead thinking about him.

The bundle was empty, except for hair. There

was no head inside it at all. Wiremu must be making monster lard on the fire, smoky monster lard out of the head. Charlie dropped the stick and backed away. He also thought that the head might have got away and be lying in wait. Perhaps the Koroua could not be killed. Or, worse still, perhaps there were several Korouas, and Elisabeth was being shared out; and what awful pudding was to follow?

On the ground, in a sort of thin grass, lay a brown bone, a small jawbone with a rank of level teeth. Elisabeth's, he thought, that is part of Liss, the small white teeth that used to smile.

At that moment the Koroua laughed, not far away, and Charlie knew the head was loose and stalking him, lying in wait, or up a tree ready to fall. In this forest there was nowhere to escape. He was bound to be caught.

He did not know what he was thinking, where he could go, or why he was here. The place had been magical for a moment, and now it was full of horrible ideas. He knew that all the ideas could not be right, but one of them must be, and none of them was a pleasant one. The choices were all bad. Even the best one, that Wiremu had killed the Koroua, meant that Elisabeth had been eaten first . . .

Surely Wiremu would not have helped to eat her . . . ? He was after all not a pakeha, and . . .

He could go wild. He might be related to the Koroua. Perhaps the bundle of hair was a baby Koroua, because no one knew how they were brought up.

Certainly there were more Korouas, because he had heard one laugh.

Now, among the small trees, feeling thin and empty and not at all well from terrifying thoughts, and in pain from his back, he thought only that something had to happen to end it all, and that it ought to happen at once.

Something happened. Elisabeth came running through the trees towards the place where Charlie had been lying. She looked at it, and then looked round for him.

She had lost all her clothes and found some more. She was dressed in the long flag leaves of New Zealand flax, dried and stitched, wound round her middle and stretched over her shoulders. No one had eaten her. Under the leaves she wore her frilly trouser-things.

"Charlie," she said, happily. "I came to get you. We are having breakfast. I have had some already. We caught a lot of fiss."

She was pleased to see him, and he was more than pleased to see her. However, he said severely, "You should be wearing your clothes." He had to be cross or start crying. He felt his eyes water, and knew it was only smoke so far that did it.

"I had to wash them," she said. "I was sick on them in the night, worse than riding in a cart."

She led him away quicker than he could go, and then helped him, small as she was. It was not far to the fire. There Wiremu was doing just what Charlie had thought, cooking fish in the smoke of a fire.

Beside the fire, sitting on a log, was a man. He had Wiremu's big knife in one hand. With the other he was tugging at his slightly long hair until he had a lock he could slice off with the knife, working round his head and beard, piece after piece. He dropped the pieces in the fire.

It was the Koroua, without his hair and most of his whiskers. It, or he, put the knife down and stood up. That made him smaller, because his legs were so short and bent. He shuffled towards Charlie.

"Oauigh," he said. Its teeth were black from eating people.

7

"He lives here," said Elisabeth. She whispered rather loudly, "He can't hear us."

"Oh yes he can," said Wiremu, turning the tail of a fish with a wooden rod. "He doesn't understand you, that's all. You right, then, Charlie? We thought you died in the night like all the fish."

The man went back to his hair-chopping, sitting on a smooth rock, looking taller again than when he was standing.

"Doesn't he understand you, either?" Charlie asked. "If he's the Koroua then he should."

"I don't know," said Wiremu. "We can all have fish again, everybody. It's all there is, and we might as well eat them."

He had a mound of fish beside him, heaped up on the tussock grass.

The Koroua understood about fish being ready. He had strange manners for a monster, because he handed Wiremu some real plates with patterns on them. Wiremu put a fish on each one, and the Koroua handed the first one to Elisabeth, and she said, "Thank you," just as if she knew how, which surprised Charlie. Generally she did not know how; but she must have known it was proper to be polite to a Koroua. It might not be fish on the plate next time, but yourself.

When Wiremu had handed out four fish he took the knife from the Koroua, just man to man, no difficulty, and gutted four more fish.

"All different kinds," he said. "Some from the sea, some from a lake; salt water and fresh water, and I don't know how, but that's what's here." And that was what he hung in the smoke.

Charlie ate his easily. The plate was a big help, and his fingers knew what to do, because they often had after fishing with Wiremu. The Koroua used his fingers too. They were not claws, and he had hands, not paws. Now and then he got a good mouthful in and then began explaining something. One use for his mouth reminded him of another.

Charlie did not know what was being said, and sometimes the Koroua did not know either, stopping to think of a word and not knowing it. He looked very much less wild with his hair cut. He also looked extremely old, which is right for a Koroua, which means Old Man, or sometimes Wild Man.

"He got the plates out of the ship," said Elisabeth, taking a bone from her mouth and dropping it into the fire. "He knew what they were. He's quite clever for a wild man."

"He knew what the knife was," said Wiremu. "My goodness, he knew. I thought I would be made into pork and baked. But the first thing he did was cut some firewood, and then he cut his hair." Wiremu waved the knife about and told the Koroua what the Koroua had done.

The Koroua waved back. He was saying words

now and then but telling a story with his arms, of how he had a knife once and had lost it a long time ago.

"Weeks and weeks," said Elisabeth.

"Woke," said the Koroua, "yeah."

There were two more fishes each, until that was enough. Then they were thirsty. The Koroua went into the water and cupped up some water in his hands. He was up to his knees in water, and began to look as if he was tall and standing deeper.

"That won't be any good," said Charlie. "It's the sea."

The Koroua found it was no good. He tasted it and spat it out.

"It's the sea," said Elisabeth. "You can't drink that. Sea."

"Sea," said the Koroua, agreeing, but thinking something was not a good idea. He looked round, probably wondering where there was drinking water.

Charlie knew. He walked slowly to the little creek and sat beside it. He could not easily bend down. He put one hand at a time into the water and drank clear fresh palmfuls, and washed his face where it felt greasy.

The Koroua climbed up into the ship. The two branches had been made into a ladder with crosspieces lashed into place very neatly with creeper stems – the leaves still grew on them. Without a ladder he could not climb easily. With it he went up, over the rail, and moved about in the ship. He made a noise, and was breaking into places.

"I think he understands ships," said Wiremu. "But he couldn't."

The Koroua understood enough to bring back what he had been looking for. He brought two cups, a metal tankard, and a pretty drinking glass with a stem. Inside the stem there was a whirl of colour. Elisabeth wanted it, so she had it. The boys had a cup each.

"It's got a pattern in it too," said Charlie, not wanting the worst thing if his sister took the best.

The Koroua kept the metal tankard. He filled it with water right to the top and drank it. He laughed, and drank again. He thought it a very great treat.

"Hold it by the handle," said Elisabeth, going to him and putting his hand in the right place. The Koroua was pleased at being corrected, and drank the next tankardful in a ridiculous and mincing way, and thought it a great joke.

It is, thought Charlie, and it is also too strange.

They sat down in the sun. The Koroua went to sleep. He left the knife beside the fire, so it was certain he had never had any idea of attacking them with it. Wiremu took it up, searched about on the little beach for the right stone, and began to put the gleam on the edge again, testing with his thumb until it was hair sharp, and then running the stone along the back to make the blade twice as sharp again. He finished that work, and went to sleep with the knife in one hand and the stone in the other.

The Koroua woke them several times by getting up to put wood on the fire. He went to sleep straight away each time, and the others only blinked awake for a moment.

When Charlie woke he first had to remember

where he was. He did not know the name of the place, but it was at the edge of the sea, somewhere round The Knuckle. He was a little disappointed that it was not home, and then felt well and strong and ready to be here, not needing Mama or Papa.

Elisabeth had put on her clothes now, and walked about like a lady. She was probably being Miss MacDonald, but Charlie knew she had no dolls to teach.

He was wrong. She had a doll made of Koroua hair, tied with more hair so that it had a neck and arms and legs and even little feet. It had a nose, which was another blob like the feet, but no eyes, and though it was made of hair it had none of its own. It was being taught to sit still, probably the only thing it knew already.

"He made it," said Elisabeth. "I think it was a goodbye present. Now he isn't here. I shall call the doll, I don't know what. Think of a name."

"Koroua," said Charlie, because it was made from that.

"No," said Wiremu. "Call it *Teleta*. Because we found that treasure ship, and if we can get it back home we shall be rich." He meant "Treasure", and nodded when Charlie guessed right.

"The divers will be rich too," said Charlie.

"Don't be silly," said Wiremu. "We've got it. They can look for a hundred years and they won't find it here. It's ours, and we'll keep it."

Charlie thought himself very stupid. I knew that, he said to his own brain. I knew it was treasure. Why did I forget?

Out in the water there was a big splashing. When they looked the Koroua was out there, swimming about, scratching at his head to make it clean, rinsing it and shaking it, and pulling at the remains of his beard.

"He needs some toothpowder," said Elisabeth severely. "Or salt like when we run out."

"You go and sit by the fire," said Wiremu. "I'm going in as well." He pulled off his shirt and began to loosen the cloth knotted round his middle, which was trousers for him.

"I'm going to play with Treasure anyway," said Elisabeth.

Charlie sat on the beach, watching her and watching the Koroua and Wiremu. Wiremu was a much better swimmer, and went down and down easily, and up again, and turned somersaults in and out of the water.

"My goodness, it was cold," he said. "The sea has changed, that's what."

Over the water there was a slow mist beginning, and the day was dying slowly. The mountains were so near that the sun was behind them long before dark. Gradually the fire took its place, and bit by bit all the world went away except what the fire saw and showed them.

"I'm hungry again," said Wiremu. "We'll have some more fish."

The Koroua had put on his flax leaves again, also the strip of them that Elisabeth had worn. He had a different idea about cooking fish for this meal. He dug a pit and rolled hot stones into it, and quite a lot of the fire too. He cleaned the fish, some with his bare hands when he forgot about the knife, and some more neatly with the knife. He wrapped them in leaves and put them on the hot stones. He laid more leaves on them, and buried them.

He sat down to wait. Elisabeth wanted to talk to him, but he did not want to talk to her. He shook his head and made noises at her when she came near.

"Just like Papa," said Charlie. "She always talks."

"He wants to be alone," said Wiremu. "I think we'll leave him alone, eh? We'll go and talk about something else. He isn't used to people all the time."

"But he must be cooking fish for us all," said Charlie. "He can't eat all that lot himself."

"Wait," said Wiremu. He went about gathering wood and dry long leaves. He went to the fire, took some of it on a stone, and carried it away. The Koroua looked at him and took no notice. Wiremu came to the ship. "Go up," he said. "We'll have a look round up there. You know what we'll see."

Charlie went up first, helped Elisabeth up, and then took the fire from Wiremu. "Just hold it," said Wiremu. He knew what he was doing, and Charlie was not sure.

"We can't burn this down," he said. "It's the *Alexander*. It's been under the sea for years."

"It's a ship," said Wiremu. "I saw where to put the fire."

He blew on the glowing coals and made a flame like a candle from a long leaf. He went into the cabin, which still stood on its iron posts with some of the roof in place, and even a few panes of glass in a rooflight.

The open deck and most of the cockpit had dried during the day's sunlight, but the cabin still had a slippery floor. "Just slow," said Wiremu, looking for what he had seen.

They all kept their backs to what lay sleeping in the berth or on the boxes.

He found it where he expected it. Sailors have to eat, and food has to be cooked. There was an iron stove, very like the range at home, with its bars at the front and the grate behind them. There was seaweedy silt hiding the spaces between the bars, but a finger or a piece of stick cleared the way.

Wiremu laid the fire in the place where fire should go, heaped small twigs on, and large, and the fire leapt up. So did smoke, but in a while it found its way out of a hole above. There was the smell of drying sea, scorching seaweed, baking mud, and at last a smell Charlie did not know he knew, of hot metal.

They went ashore for more wood. The fire began to make its own roaring noise and to send out its own stars to match those in the sky, and its own mist to join the vapours across the water.

"It's a very quiet sea," said Wiremu. "When's high tide? This is a very low one. I don't understand it."

"Our house," said Elisabeth, happy with that until she thought of Mama and the proper way for the day to end.

Wiremu made a torch, binding dry flax leaves together on a stick, like a great feather duster. When it was ready he lit it.

"Now for the treasure," he said, leading them to the hold.

All the water had run out of the cabin. The middle of it was filled with boxes, packed tight and nailed firmly, with iron straps round them. Wiremu and Charlie began to push and pull at the wood and iron, trying to move or open the boxes.

The iron did not give. The wood sat firm and unrotted, nothing wrong with it. None of the boxes would move. They stopped trying, not feeling so strong as usual.

"There's this old fellow," said Charlie, feeling brave. "We should take him on land, eh?" He came back with the skull and laid it on the deck. Its eyes were black. He went back for the jawbones.

"Don't like it," said Elisabeth.

"Don't start," said Charlie, very firmly. "Only a sailor."

"Loose teeth," said Wiremu. "We'll get him on land, that's where sailors are making for."

With his finger-tips he helped Charlie hold the bones.

Then the Koroua was calling for them, "Hoo, hoo," and they went to him. Charlie was thinking of coming back in daylight, a better time for bones. He carried the skull and the jaws, and felt sorry for what the man had been.

The Koroua took the bones straight from Charlie's hands. "Da, da," he said. And he looked at what he held, reaching out one hand to draw the torch nearer.

When he looked back again into Charlie's eyes, on a level with his own as they both stood, his eyes were full of tears, tears that dropped and dropped into the eye sockets of the skull. The Koroua tried to speak a word he knew, but it would not come. Instead of it there was a sob, because he was holding a friend.

Elisabeth went to stand near him, and rested her head on him too, wanting to comfort him and be comforted herself.

Wiremu went to wash his hands after touching private things like bones, or even thinking of them.

8

Tears ran down the Koroua's face. He held the skull and looked into its eyes. He knew who it was. He spoke to it, but the reply was too far away in time to be heard.

It is his friend, thought Charlie.

"It is his Papa," said Elisabeth. "It has made him sad."

It is someone he has eaten, thought Charlie. His teeth are black. "But how could he have been on the ship?" he said out loud.

Wiremu was coming back from rinsing his hands after touching bones. He did not look at the skull again, thinking it should not be seen at all.

"It was bad luck," he said, crossly. "We are here. That is bad luck." 'Pata roke,' was the way he said it. Elisabeth did not understand him.

The Koroua put the skull out of sight. He smiled at them. He was not sad, exactly. He rubbed his cheeks, wiping away tears, and smoothing down his beard. He smoothed his arms too, where strong feelings of surprise and wonder had made the hair rise and the skin roughen.

He was happy in some strange way, as if he knew at last what had happened to someone he knew, as if he belonged to the world again. He looked round the place they were in, among rocks with the fire making it home, at the stars beginning above, at the trees by the water's edge, at the ship. He understood something more. He gave a great shiver, and began to uncover the place where the fish was cooking.

"No," said Wiremu, turning his back on the Koroua and getting in his way at the same time. "I am doing that. Your hands are not clean. *Korutu* is *tapu*." He pointed to where the skull was now hidden. "Go and wash them." He rubbed his own hands together to show what he meant.

The Koroua blinked and blinked, until Elisabeth led him away to the creek. "I shall wash mine too," she said. "So there."

When she came back Charlie and Wiremu were lifting long leaves from the ground. They were not burned, but cooked, and the fish wrapped inside them baked soft and sweet. She had brought the plates from where she had left them in the water after the last meal. "But I do not want any," she said, until she smelt and saw. Then she ate as easily as she had before.

After that they sat in the dark round the fire, with the sky shivering at their backs. The night before they had not cared what happened. On this night they felt cold, and a wind was roaming about the trees, talking a little as it came and went, bringing the taste of ice down from the high peaks.

Only the Koroua sat comfortable, with his crooked legs in front of him, eating the last of the fish and throwing the bones to crackle in the fire.

The stars came out, and then they went away.

The moon glowed as it rose. It was shaded by racing clouds, then pushed behind them, and at last blown out by the wind.

Rain began to fall, a few drops like sparks on the skin, then a steady shower, making the fire pale with blackness and hissing into steam.

The Koroua valued his fire more than anything. He got up, built the fire larger with pieces of tree, then began to bury it under soil and clods of grassy earth that he pulled from the ground. In the end the fire had gone out of sight in its own little house. Only its steamy smoke came out from cracks and joins, smelling of hot clay.

There was no heat now, and the rain grew colder and stronger. The Koroua hunched himself down to sit through it. He seemed used to it. He did not mind being wet and cold if his fire lived for another day.

"We'll go on the ship again," said Charlie, holding Elisabeth close. She was shivering and unhappy, and looking for her doll. "Treasure," she said. "I want Treasure." She found him at her feet. "He feels like grass," she said.

"*Teleta*," said Wiremu, his Maori word for treasure. "We have a fire and a roof on the ship. It is the best place."

It was a difficult place to get to in complete darkness. There was nothing to help them on the way. It was so dark that Charlie could sense the side of the ship in front of him all the time, but not feel it with outstretched hands. He walked slowly sideways with his head tipped forward, waiting for it to be banged. He knew the ship would be hard on his head, even if his hands went through the side.

They climbed up the Koroua's ladder and on to a deck that seemed as steep as a roof now, ready to slide them off into the water if they let go.

Wiremu found the fire by putting his hand in it. "Ayee," he said. "There is burning," and he blew on the burning and made an ember red hot. It was already better under the remains of the cabin roof, out of the way of most of the wind and rain.

Wiremu teased the fire into life. The smoke began to go up the stump of chimney again, and rain came down in spits and hisses. Wiremu went off by himself for more wood. "You look after Itapeta," he told Charlie. Elisabeth was asleep in Charlie's arms, and Treasure was asleep in hers.

They kept the fire going all night, and the night kept the rain falling. After that the day kept it falling still. The water lay flat under it, only raised into gooseflesh by the rain everywhere on it.

"It is flattening the waves," said Wiremu, looking out from the cockpit, half sheltered in the cabin still. "It is not like the sea we know."

"He said it was sea," said Elisabeth. "He told me."

"It is a very little tide," said Wiremu. He had been noticing, he said. The tide came up a foot, and then went down a foot, and that was all. It was not the behaviour of the sea, he said.

"We are a long way from the open water," said Charlie. "What about breakfast?"

"I know what to do," said Charlie.

Elisabeth had been awake for some time, staying by the fire and finding some iron doors close by it. They were oven doors. She rubbed them with a leaf, and managed to open one door.

70

There was nothing much in it but rust on all sides, and a tipped shelf. A lump on a corner of the shelf was a pie dish with something in it, some long-forgotten meal that had gone down with the wreck. But there was warmth in the oven, and Charlie had so often seen Mama making her oven work that he knew what to do.

"You pull out a damper," he said, for once knowing far more than Wiremu. "And the fire goes round that way and makes the oven hot."

The damper was there, but firmly locked in. He had to hit it for a long time with a stone from the shore. But at last it moved and he drew it out.

He knew at once why it was called a damper. Behind it there was a flood of black water, which came racing round behind the oven, made straight for the fire, and put it completely out.

"It doesn't do that at home," said Charlie. "This one is old and does not work properly."

"It does not matter," said Wiremu. "I will fetch some from the Koroua's fire."

He was gone a long time, and then he came back empty-handed. "We shall go fishing," he said. "Where is my spear?"

It was in the hold. Wiremu banged at the boxes in there with its end before taking it away. "All the fish that were dead have gone bad," he said. "We must catch some more. The Koroua has gone to find some of his own. He has buried his fire, and I dare not open the ground. It is raining *pipi* everywhere."

He went to look for bait, digging in the rough sand with his bare hands. He came back with some ugly worms.

71

"They are not right," he said. "But the fish will not know, perhaps. Where is your line?"

They sat in the rain at the end of the ship, waiting for something to tug at the lines. Nothing came. Only dead fish, beginning to smell, floated on the water. Now and then there would be a bubble on the water as a fish already dead came to the surface, gasping for air and not getting it.

A long time later the Koroua came walking along the edge of the water, carrying one small thing. His home-made line was round his shoulder, and a white hook, like a bird-bone, pinned his leaves together. He carried one small bird and no fish.

Elisabeth might have felt hungry, but she did not say so. She spent her time housekeeping by the fire, now and then putting some more wood on the dead ashes, talking to neighbours, and looking in cupboards. She was looking for the cakes, she said, and being a shop.

When the Koroua came back she had found things to rattle in the bottom of a tipped and twisted cupboard. Charlie went to see what it all was, and found her eating, or pretending to, the pudding in the dish from the oven, using a black spoon. She had found spoons and forks and the white handles of knives. Charlie thought the forks and spoons were silver, because they were so heavy. "Gold," said Elisabeth.

The Koroua came aboard. He had already seen the fireplace and thought it was useless. He shook his head at it. He looked round again, and shook his head at everything.

"He has not been on this ship," said Wiremu.

"He has," said Charlie. But he could not be sure.

Perhaps the skull did not belong to a friend or relative, but had just made the Koroua sad to see such a thing.

The Koroua looked at the knives and forks, and at a broken saucer Elisabeth had found. He tried a fork, knowing how to hold it, but there was nothing to stick it into.

In the end he left the ship and went into the rain again. He beckoned them to follow him, and they did. He led them to the fireplace again. He undid one end of the fire and put the bird, a duck, to cook, complete with its feathers, turning it round until they had burnt away. He brushed off the remaining black smelly cinders, and slit the bird open with Wiremu's knife to take out the parts no one eats.

"That might make bait," said Wiremu, taking the guts away. "We'll just try again."

But they still caught nothing. And they began to realize that the edge of the water was beginning to smell, because there were so many dead fish floating on the surface or left at the edge. There were flies, and flies' eggs on the fish.

Elisabeth came for them. She was wet through but did not care. "The goose is cooked," she said.

The duck was ready. There were plates for it, and forks for a polite meal, but one small wild duck among four people does not make a meal. They were still hungry afterwards.

The Koroua made a bundle of twigs, and then a bundle of larger branches. He tied them with creeper. He opened up the fire and brought out pebbles of charcoal. He heaped them into the bundle of larger wood, buried the fire again with great care, took up his two bundles, and was ready to go somewhere.

He gave the knife to Wiremu, the four plates to Charlie, the forks and spoons to Elisabeth, looked round to say goodbye to this place, and walked off. He paused just round the corner and picked up the skull. He checked to see that everyone was following, and went on his way again.

"I expect he knows best," said Charlie. "He might take us back to Jade Bay. We can come back for the treasure."

They went slowly. The Koroua, on his crooked legs, could not move fast at all. Walking was not only difficult, but gave him pain as well. Now and then he had to stop and hold his leg when some sort of cramp took hold. There was nothing to be done to help him, except see that the coals of fire in the bundle stayed alight, being fed with a damp twig now and then. The smoke wreathed about them as they went.

They were going up a mountain, on a difficult path between rocks and trees. At some places the Koroua had to sit himself down and hoist himself along with his hands up tall steps. The journey took a long time.

At one moment they reached the top of the track, but not the top of the mountain. They began to go downwards again, but no faster, in another valley full of trees.

"It's as quick as me," said Elisabeth, picking her way just as awkwardly as the Koroua, clutching the cutlery in one hand and Treasure in the other.

"*Rorirori*," said Wiremu, not knowing the English for clumsy. "And we are going nowhere."

In a few yards the smoke from the fire began to be lighter, to burn more warmly. The rain had stopped now they were into the next valley, and sunshine began to dry them and their clothes.

They came round a corner, following the Koroua. He went on walking at the same slow pace. He did not pause or look back, but went sideways into a shadow under a rock and vanished.

They stood and waited. In the shadow, after a few minutes, there was blue smoke, and then the glow of fire. There was more than shadow. There was the darkness of a cave. "Hoo, hoo," said the Koroua, and it seemed he was inviting them in.

"That's where they all live," said Wiremu. "They must live somewhere. "I'm not going in."

"Hoo, hoo," said the Koroua again. But he was not talking to them. Other voices answered him, shouting from not far away.

9

Charlie at first was sure the voices belonged to people they knew. He thought for a moment that he recognized the cough of the man at the telegraph office, Siggy Webber.

He knew they were not the voices of people when they came out into the open air, trying to run out of the cave but not succeeding. They were the voices of sheep. They were not able to run free because they had straps round their shoulders, tied above them to knobbly rope, and the other end of the rope was held by the Koroua.

The sheep came out as headlong as they could, pulling the Koroua, helping him along faster than he could go.

Charlie understood why the ropes were necessary. A badly crippled man would have great difficulty getting close to a sheep if he could not run, and had no dog. When he had captured a sheep he would have to put it on a lead, like the dog he hadn't got, to keep it where he wanted.

The sheep were only used to the Koroua. "Keep still," Charlie said to Elisabeth, who had begun to jump up and down. The sheep started to run off in all directions, one actually falling over when it reached the end of the rope that held it, others trying to go in two or three directions at once, the smallest one leaping into the air and landing on its back where it wriggled like a beetle.

"They skairt of you," said Wiremu. "Big falait." Big fright, he meant. Some sheep thought they would go back into their nice safe cave, and were ready to trample on the Koroua. He was very strong, and fought back, shortening and shortening the ropes until the whole flock, which was only about nine animals but made enough fuss for ninety, had to stand still, looking wild, panting, hating their neighbours, stamping their feet, and trying to grab a mouthful from a bush.

"Hoo, hoo," called the Koroua, to calm them. They rolled their eyes at him, and gradually grew used to everything round them. That was what sheep did, Charlie thought. You can't tell what pleases them, but they are better than goats.

The Koroua freed one of his hands, and waved it at Charlie to make him sit down while things were sorted out.

"Better do it," said Charlie, sitting down and pulling Elisabeth on to his knee to hold her. "You can stroke them later," he told her, because that was what she wanted to do.

The Koroua tied the sheep one by one to trees among the rocks. He went around and counted them, then took Wiremu's knife and cut branches for them to chew on.

"There's only one Koroua," said Charlie. "I thought he was bringing all of them out. I thought they all lived here, maybe dozens of them."

"The others will be along," said Wiremu. "Bound to be, you know how it is with Korouas."

Charlie did not know. He used to think that Wiremu had made them up, until he met one. Wiremu could still be making up the rest of them, of course.

When his work was done the Koroua invited them into the cave. It was his house.

There was a big old fire in it, much larger than anything he could have made since getting here. In fact the fire he had brought in the bundle of sticks from beside the water was still lying on a stone, burning separately.

"Somebody was here," said Charlie. "Keeping the fire going while he was out."

But there was no one in here now. There was only one room to the cave, with the place where the sheep had been tied at the back, a wooden cage made from branches. The fire was in the middle towards the front. On one side there was the Koroua's bed, made from springier branches and sheep's wool, soft but smelly. On the other was a deep and wide ledge where he kept things. Wiremu examined it carefully for secret doors, or other mischief.

"They might work magic on us," he said. "But if they are it's one that makes them invisible, so there's nothing we can do."

"I like our one," said Elisabeth. "My Koroua."

The high roof was black with smoke, making a chimney where most of the smoke went.

There were no more Korouas. Wiremu thought they might be up in the chimney, because of some

78

Maori story he had heard, but that did not seem likely, with so much smoke there.

"Some of our heroes would not sneeze," said Wiremu. He had to explain himself many times, until Charlie knew what his words meant.

The Koroua sat by the fire for a time. He handed the knife back to Wiremu, showing with his thumb where it was no longer sharp. Wiremu went outside and found a stone that would set matters right.

The Koroua showed them what he had used instead of a knife. He had made tools out of stone, worn smooth and black, or polished right through and richly golden, with slice-sharp edges. He showed them how he did that, hitting stone on stone.

He put his fishing line and hook on the broad shelf, the knotted length and the hook white as bone. It was that, Charlie found, looking at it. He was not allowed to touch it.

"They take a lot of making," said Wiremu. "With a stone knife."

Some of the other things on the shelf were unknown to them, but others were easily understood. There were wooden bowls, not very round, but hollowed out by stone knives. There were hammers of bone. There were candles, but not so neat as shop ones, and also mouldy. There was one wooden plate, and a spoon made of bone.

The Koroua put the plates, cups, the glass and the tankard, the silver spoons and the forks, on the shelf, and was very pleased.

He told them to sit where they were, by the fire, and went out again. He took the sharpened knife

79

with him. When he came in he was carrying bundles of branches, which he dumped in the entrance. He said some words, but was not sure of them when no one understood. But he pointed to his own bed and to the bundles he had brought, and they understood they had to make one up for themselves, just there, where he pointed, close against the sheep pen.

Next he brought a bundle of sheep's wool, to cover and soften the bed. Charlie had often seen sheep-shearing, but never with a stone knife, the only sort the Koroua had.

"It has not been cut," said Wiremu, looking at the lengths of wool. "He has pulled the wool off when it has broken. It does that every year."

Charlie went on helping him to make the bed. Elisabeth was making pillows of some mossy stuff. She was so busy and happy at it that Charlie was pleased, because she was so awful when she was cross.

But all at once she looked round and said, "Is that right, Mama?" and found that Mama was not there. She was homesick at once and began to cry for Mama and cups of tea, "and tables," she said. "Why don't they have any tables?"

They were alone in the monster's cave, making a bed, Charlie realized. "It is not a bed," he said miserably, filled with sadness himself. "It is like the story and he is going to eat us. This is a pie and in the night he will bake us."

"You can go to sleep on a *hangi* pit," said Wiremu, talking about the hole where hot stones baked the food. "It's warm, but don't let the women catch you."

The Koroua came in with firewood, and went out with something from the shelf. He brought that back and stood it carefully where it had been. It was a bowl of milk, still warm.

"Cows too," said Charlie.

"Sheep," said Wiremu.

There were several more journeys. Each was a lot of work for the Koroua, with his difficulty in walking. He whistled at first, and could be heard talking to something outside, which turned out to be the sheep, not other Korouas. But as he came and went, and saw his visitors becoming more and more sad, he stopped whistling, and became unhappy himself.

In the end there was darkness outside and fire-light inside. He came and stood by the fire.

"Hoo," he said softly, and moved his arms to make his new companions sit round the fire too. He stuck a straight branch across the fire, putting his end on an upright post, and pointing to another at Charlie's end. Charlie put his end there, and realized that there were pieces of meat on the branch, roasting in the glow.

At one edge of the fire the Koroua had buried something. He dug them out now, handed round plates and spoons, and gave them a roasted root each. He had one himself. While the roots cooled he dipped each of them a drink of milk, Charlie and Wiremu having cups, Elisabeth having her glass with the pretty stem, and the Koroua using the metal tankard.

"Wait a minute," said Charlie, after making a small hole in his root, smelling the sweet flesh inside, and before tasting it. "We have to say Grace."

They all stood up, the Koroua seeming to know what was happening.

"If I can remember it," said Charlie. "Grandpa used to say it, when he was alive. 'Danke, lieber Gott, für . . . für' something. Oh, I can't remember."

But the Koroua was remembering. His eyes opened wide, and he was thinking, recalling. "Danke," he said, rustily, "lieber Gott," and he went on speaking, still rustily, some more words that might be right, but which Charlie could not understand. But the Koroua could not get it all back and say it. Charlie thought it was strange if he knew it at all; and he was sure the Koroua had only repeated his own words and then lost his way.

They all sat down and opened up the root. It was some sort of sweet potato, hot into the mouth, cooled by a sip of milk, and chewed creamy with it, going down to a grateful stomach.

After it there was meat, which had gradually darkened and dropped fat that flamed in the embers, until the meat itself was purring gently to itself. One piece dropped into the fire, but the Koroua ate that himself. The rest he shared out, crisp as toast, and hotter.

After that there was more. He brought down one of the lumps from the shelf, put it on a flat stone, and cut it down into quarters. There was a thick green skin of mould, then a springy yellow layer, and inside a firm creamy whiteness. It was cheese, bitter with a different sort of salt, but as good as the cheese sometimes was in the store, in the times when it was not very good. Charlie had eaten worse, especially when no one would buy it and it had to be eaten at home.

After that the Koroua sent them to bed. He spent a long time heaping the fire up and putting that to bed too, covering it and making it safe. He took some of it outside and made a careful fire there.

"He always makes a copy," said Wiremu. "There was still fire when we got here, but he carried some as well. He is making another outside in case this one goes out."

"I thought other Korouas had kept it alight," said Charlie.

"Oh," said Wiremu, "They'll come tomorrow, you'll see."

The next day, however, nothing much happened. The Koroua brought back fruit for breakfast, going out before anyone else was awake. Then he took them to the sheep, which he moved one by one, each to another tree, pulling branches for them, gathering grass and weeds for them, taking a bowl of water round, filled from a little trickle of water near the cave.

At first Charlie thought he was very kindly entertaining them, letting them help, a week-end on a farm.

When the Koroua had done it once or twice he expected Charlie to do the next sheep, Wiremu the one after, and Elisabeth the next. Charlie thought it was still kind of him, until Wiremu pointed out that they were now working and had been given jobs.

83

"Well, it's not much," said Charlie. "We can do a bit for him."

"He's nice to us," said Elisabeth. "I would like to be at home, but I like working. It's better than school when Miss MacDonald is cross."

The next day Charlie was taught to milk the sheep. Three of them were giving milk for the Koroua, and three others were raising the next three, now well-grown lambs. The tenth, because there were ten, did nothing except eat and complain.

Elisabeth was being taught to cook on the open fire. Wiremu was sent for firewood. There were also other things, like carrying stones down to the cave. The Koroua wanted another building, they understood.

"I told you it was work," said Wiremu. "It's worse than school. At least that ends at the end of the day, and not *Hatarei*." Saturday, he meant.

"I think I know what it is," said Charlie, on the third day, when he was having to cut up some sour milk and pour off the clear liquid, which he found was most of supper that night. The solid parts were to make cheese.

"Slaves," said Wiremu. "*Tiuti*." He meant duty.

"No," said Charlie. "Slaves do all the work there is. He is still doing work. But he is not going to take us back to Jade Bay. He is going to keep us. He thinks we are his family. He thinks we are all the other Korouas. That is what he thinks, and that is what we are."

"No," said Wiremu. "Never. I will not be a Koroua."

84

"Then what shall we do?" said Charlie. "We can't get away alone. We are going to be here for ever, and we don't know where that is."

10

The Koroua had a little garden. He had dug it with a stick, and taken out all the stones. Charlie and Wiremu had to carry the big ones to the cave. Any little ones had been thrown away. The soil was easy to dig now, and grew roots, and other things the Koroua had found tasty and safe.

"I don't know what they are," said Wiremu. "We just grow pakeha stuff now, riki, pi, tupeka, parete, aporo, heki." He was sure those were the English words for onions, peas, tobacco, potatoes, apples, and eggs, and of course Charlie understood him. When they had moved the stones they could carry, or roll, then Elisabeth was made the gardener, and told what were weeds, and how to pick caterpillars off the crops and squash them with her fingers.

One day the Koroua went out early, leaving them to their work. For a change they all did each other's jobs, taking grubs from the leaves, foraging for the sheep, bringing them water, moving one very big stone and then resting, milking the sheep in the afternoon, and tidying up the cave a great deal when there was rain outside.

They did not touch the fire. The Koroua had

left it heaped high with wet clayey soil, and it smouldered bitterly like a huge smoky tortoise, humped in the middle of the cave. If it had been a tortoise shell two of them could have curled up inside it.

"We could go home," Charlie said to Wiremu, at a moment when Elisabeth was not near. "We could just walk out."

"He doesn't want us," said Wiremu. "Nobody wants *tamariki*." He meant children. "They make big noise and much dust, like Itapeta." Elisabeth was sweeping the floor with a bundle of twigs and singing to herself. She was home already.

"Mama wants me," said Charlie. "And Itapeta. We could go when he isn't looking."

"We could go any time," said Wiremu. "What stops us?"

"We don't know where to go," said Charlie. "That's all. We can't see out to anywhere, and we don't know where we are." He thought of Miss MacDonald and the map of the world with the white part in the middle, where the spider lived, perhaps. Perhaps they were in the white bit, he suggested to Wiremu.

"No," said Wiremu. "We're in The Knuckle. Nobody goes there either. There's no way in and no way out."

Charlie thought there was something else that Wiremu was thinking about The Knuckle, but Wiremu went away then to look at the sheep, in spite of the rain. Charlie thought he did not want to be asked anything. A Maori could be a friend, he decided, but this was their land first, and they had secret thoughts about it that pakehas could not share. It was not right to ask about such things. That, Papa once said, led to missionaries being eaten and tooth decay among the Maoris.

Charlie remembered the treasure later on, and wondered whether Wiremu had been keeping that to himself. Wiremu had forgotten about treasure, he said. "It's pakeha *teleta*," he said. "We wouldn't want it. But I will help you get it."

"I'd like to get it first, and then, you know, we could do what we thought." He did not want Elisabeth to know in case she told the Koroua and everything else that could hear. No one knew what the Koroua understood.

"I'll stay here," said Elisabeth. She could understand the Koroua without words, and Charlie whatever he said.

There was cold meat to eat that night. They left a helping for the Koroua. They went to bed and to sleep when it was the right time. In the morning the Koroua was back. Of course he could not say where he had been, but he had a string of fish to bake, and some fruit too sour to eat. The juice turned milk sour at once, leaving it full of threads. The Koroua liked that. The fruit also turned their teeth black, which interested the Koroua very much. Elisabeth was able to tell him that his teeth were black too. She made quite certain that he knew later in the day.

The Koroua went to sleep for a while, then came out to see that everything was running properly. When he had done that he began to dig a hole in a place that he liked, choosing it with care, considering whether the sun shone on it most of the day, and that it was sheltered from rain. When he had dug deep, as far as he could reach, and made the bottom of the hole smooth, he laid flat stones all round the hole, in a square, and had another flat stone to cover the hole itself.

He went to wash his hands and to tidy himself, asking whether his hair was evenly cut, his beard respectable. He sent all three of them off to become tidy too, and waited for them.

He had brought the skull from the ship and wished to bury it. He brought it out and carried it to its grave very solemnly. He was not unhappy any more, but proud to have found someone he knew. He explained by pointing that the front teeth, a little crooked and crossing, told him who it was. It was then that Elisabeth showed him finally that its teeth were white, and his own black, like Charlie's. "Liss," said Charlie, but the Koroua did not mind. Only Wiremu stayed back a little.

"He was my friend," said the Koroua, but not in words, and then with one word, "Ernst," buried him, with the view to look at, the spring of water to hear, the sun to rest in, patting him down tight with handfuls of earth. They all helped, and at the last the hole was covered with one stone. The Koroua went off into his garden alone to think about things.

He came back with some blue flowers, filled his tankard with water, put the flowers in, and set them on the grave. Elisabeth went off herself and picked flowers of another kind, and put them in her glass beside the tankard.

"He would have been our friend too," she said.

"We can't go," said Charlie, a day or two later. "We are all one family now." The burial of the skull had joined them all together, and Charlie felt that he had always been here, and perhaps always would be.

"But nobody lives here," said Wiremu, when he had thought it out a bit.

Charlie looked at the Koroua. At this very moment he was making a wooden comb for Elisabeth, cutting slowly with the knife. He was sure her hair should be tidy. "Ha," he said, when he had finished. "Elisabett."

Elisabeth obediently combed her hair. It took a long time, because it was full of knots. At the end of it the comb had fallen to pieces, but the hair was tamed. The Koroua cut another, and put it at the back of the shelf. It was not to be used yet.

"You see," said Charlie.

Then they had a holiday. One morning the Koroua brought the sheep in. Charlie and Wiremu had to spend a long time filling a trough in the cave with water. Elisabeth had to bring dried grass and leaves from a stack beyond the garden, and a great deal of new leaves too. The sheep were tied in to their place. The fire was stacked tight with wood and clamped down with another great mound of wet clay, this time a giant tortoise. This empty shell Charlie and Wiremu and Elisabeth could all three have slept in. It was plain that they were going somewhere. Some embers were kept aside to be carried away with them.

They took no food. They would find it on the way, the Koroua said, in his descriptive waving of arms, and they set off. There was no door to close, no one who understood goodbye, only the complaints of sheep, but they complained all day to one another or anyone passing.

"We have been this way," said Wiremu, after a time, as they followed the Koroua at Koroua's pace, which was slow. "Last time it was raining."

"We have only been in one other place," said Charlie. "We'll get to the treasure again. I wish it wasn't so heavy, because we'll never carry it."

Wiremu was right about the way they came. At last they began to see a glimmer of something through the trees, where the water lay.

"It's the sea again," said Elisabeth. "We'll go fissing."

"We go where the food is," said Wiremu.

The Koroua stopped to gather a dry twig and keep his bundle of fire healthy. It was like a pet to him, and he took more notice of fire than of almost anything else. He was always waking in the night to look, and feed the embers, and always laid a fire out beside the garden to sleep the night there. He would tend that fire day and night too.

Now the smoke went down with them to the waterside. It mingled with a sea-side smell, but not agreeably. Charlie wondered what the Koroua was burning.

"Sea," said the Koroua.

"I told him that word," said Elisabeth, glad to have a pupil. She quickly taught it to Treasure. She said he knew it ever so well.

Then she was running into the water, pulling off her stockings and shoes, and prancing over the shingle and gritty sand, squealing at the prickliness and at the cold.

The Koroua went to the same fireplace. He had

buried a fire here too, and it was still burning from his last visit. Elisabeth came back to warm her feet at it.

Charlie had looked at the fire, watched Elisabeth, picked up her shoes, and then remembered the ship. He knew where it was, and he expected to see it. But he remained staring at the place because the ship was not there. He knew he was stupid, but kept on looking, as if it would appear on being stared for. But it was not there.

Wiremu had looked once, and then searched better. He saw the black shape further off to the right, and not on the shore at all. It seemed to be floating some way out, and perhaps moving a little. That might have been an effect of the slowly rippling water, disturbed by Elisabeth.

She had come out of the water because it was cold, and because it was slippery. "And smelly," she said. "It is so smelly."

It was smelly. There was nothing but the smell of dead fish, with no smoke to disguise it. The reason was clear. There were heaps of dead fish at the water's edge, their bones showing, and things wriggling among them. The lapping of waves broke them open, or set them floating. There were flies busy everywhere.

Elisabeth cleaned her feet with leaves, and still they smelt.

The Koroua was not worried. He knew what he was doing and why he had come. He told them all to be quiet, and sat on a headland in the stench of dead fish, and listened. The Koroua sharpened the knife slowly, stroke, stroke, stroke, dulling the singing noise by pressing the back of the blade on his poor knee.

After a long time, and after he had hushed Elisabeth several times and made her cross, he cocked his ear, because he had heard something.

Somewhere down the water something was rustling and grunting a little. Along the shore something moved.

"Korouas," said Charlie. "They will be."

"*Puaka*," said Wiremu. He was right. The Maoris say porker, for the pigs Captain Cook left in their country. Black against the silvery sunset water the pigs had come to feed on rotting fish. The humans would feed on the pigs.

The Koroua did nothing. He waited. He had expected the pigs. He seemed happy to watch them and to do nothing.

But now Charlie understood why there was a particularly strong pole of wood beside the fireplace, firm enough for a pig. But something has to be done to catch the pig, and the Koroua was doing nothing.

He did not have to. He had done his work a day or two before. All at once the pigs started to one side and grunted snufflingly. But one of them was beyond mere grunting. It was squealing and shouting, and making a very dreadful fuss. The others bent up their ugly heads and looked at something up in a tree.

"Hoo," said the Koroua. He took the knife up. He had expected the noise to follow the pigs. The pigs had not. After a discussion they went away, all except the one who was still singing out.

It had been trapped in a noose, and was hanging

by both back legs in a tree, a rope swinging near it. If the other pigs had known how they would have lowered it to the ground. The Koroua asked Charlie and Wiremu to do that, and waited under the pig for it. When it came down it squealed even more loudly, and then stopped. The Koroua walked out into the lake to rinse some pig blood from himself and the knife. The rest of the blood ran down into the forest.

Two hours later, in the dark, Charlie was eating crackling and the warm juice was running down his chin. The pig slept over the fire, and the knife went from hand to hand as a slice was wanted.

They were still eating in the morning. But the Koroua had gone.

"He has taken a leg with him," said Elisabeth, being the Mama at the outdoor kitchen.

"To eat, not to walk on," said Charlie.

"Is he safe alone?" asked Elisabeth, being the Mama to all these men.

"Are we?" said Wiremu. "There is no cave."

"We'll go and live on the boat," said Charlie. That's it. You, me, and Liss."

"Sail, sail, sail," said Elisabeth, forgetting household cares.

11

Elisabeth sat by the fire alone while Charlie and Wiremu pulled fallen wood out from under the trees and launched it into the water. She had not come with them when they tried to walk out to the ship. She could still smell yesterday, she said.

The ship was beyond walking depth. Wiremu was ready to swim the short distance, but Charlie had pointed out, in the end, that they would have to get the treasure on shore and it wouldn't swim with them.

"*Moki*," said Wiremu. He did not know the English word for a raft, but soon made a twiggy model as big as his hand. Charlie had laughed at it, because it seemed so sweet and impossible for them to travel on anything so small. He knew it was a model, and that they had to make a bigger one, but he felt light-headed and strange. He thought it was the excitement of treasure, and not having to work with the sheep or toil shifting stone.

They built the *moki* on the sour shore, length by length, tying the irregular branches with new creepers and the longest flax leaves they could find. The *moki* was pushed out on the water as they made it. It sank at first, and Charlie thought it was hopeless, and wanted to stop. Wiremu made him work on and on. It was worse than working at the cave, but at least they were making something for themselves. They had the hope, too, of finding the gold and silver and the copper coins still shining, somehow like a pain behind the eyes.

"I can buy things any time," said Charlie, "because I live in the store." He shook his head, reminded of the store and thinking about sugary sweets and wishing he had not.

"You live in The Knuckle," said Wiremu. "We all do."

"But we're leaving," said Charlie. How they were leaving was not clear. In any case, what they were doing now was going to live on the ship.

"They will come for us," said Charlie. He thought that would happen, and that it would have to. Here they were at the end of a finger of sea, and a boat would come sailing in among the mountains.

The raft floated, but as deep as water, sunk, but not below the surface. It moved about, but not very exactly, when Wiremu poled it with a long trunk from a young tree.

"I'll go and get her," said Charlie.

"Bring some fire," said Wiremu. "I will collect firewood."

Elisabeth left the fire slowly. "I want to stay here," she said. She was thinking what Charlie thought, that someone would come for them. "Then they'll be able to find me better."

She came to the raft fretfully, and looked at it

with disdain. "It has sinked already," she said, seeing it lying level with the surface of the water.

They got her on it, and she stood rolling her eyes. "It isn't flat," she said, her foot slipping through a gap.

Charlie thought he should pole. Wiremu held the fire in a basket of sticks on a stone. Elisabeth sat on the stack of firewood. The ship waited for them about fifty feet away.

Charlie got the pole into the sand down below, and heaved. Nothing happened. He expected the *moki* to slide through the water, so that he could snatch the pole up and push again with it as they moved. He was left to push against the bottom of the water, push, push, push, and the *moki* seemed not to move.

"It's stuck, he said. "It's gone aground."

"Keep on," said Wiremu.

Gradually, then more quickly, and at last too fast, the *moki* moved. Charlie hauled at the pole, pulled it from the sand below, and waited to thrust it in again.

"It's given me a stitch," he said, because there was a pain in his side. It was a bad stitch, and he let go of the pole to hold himself. In a few seconds the pain was more than a stitch. It was more like a row of nails being driven into him. He could not stand up, and fell down on the watery top of the raft, curled up and hardly able to breathe. The pain sawed through him like a living thing, biting, scratching, tearing.

"Carry the fire," Wiremu said to Elisabeth, handing it to her. But she could not take it. She could not see it because she was crying, and her hands were holding her own self because she had the pain too.

The pole dropped into the water and floated away on another voyage. Wiremu was not certain what to rescue, the pole or the fire, and in the end had neither. The fire dropped into the water, and the pole went back to land. The *moki* sat where it was, turning round and round slowly, between the ship and the shore. Wiremu stood and waited to see what happened.

"Mama," said Elisabeth. "Mama, I am here. I feel sick, Mama." She sobbed, face up watching for comfort and not getting it. Tears ran in a flood on her face. She tried to scream, but taking enough breath was too painful.

Charlie felt he could not move. He felt cold water taking his strength away, but he did not care. He was unable to help himself at all. The pain inside him was like a separate thing that he had to hold, something living and with a mind of its own, busily burning his insides out.

He had felt light-headed earlier, but he had not known that pain would follow. He felt guilty too about letting the pain get to Elisabeth. She had felt very quiet all day, sitting by the fire and doing nothing; he knew that she did that at home when she was sickening for anything, and he had not cared. So his mind, as well as his gut, was biting him.

Wiremu's dark skin began to have a greenish look. He no longer looked happy, and was biting back some uneasy feelings. He took a breath, faltering a little as he did so when a twinge of some sort struck across him. He went over the side of the raft and began to push it to the shore.

Then all at once he too could do nothing. He was taken by a sudden cramp, and it was all he could do to hold on to the raft to save himself. It was beyond him to climb aboard again.

Charlie reached out a hand really needed for himself. He clutched Wiremu's wrist, and held him.

The *moki* drifted on its own. No one belonging to it was strong enough to push or pull it anywhere.

Charlie became sick and ill. He heard Elisabeth choking in the same way and then stop. He was sure she was dead, and that he would be the same very soon. Wiremu floated on his back now, but seemed to have stopped breathing.

The *moki* turned and turned, slow as the sun overhead.

I have been taken on a hook, Charlie thought. I have swallowed it and it is being pulled out, but through my belly, not my mouth.

There was a short time when the pain was less, and he was able to sit up. Elisabeth was hunched over beside the firewood, sitting in water, her head now bowed. Her clothes would have to be washed again, every one, but she was breathing in a shallow way. Wiremu was trying to climb aboard, so slowly that Charlie thought he had stopped trying. Charlie was able to pull him further on, and then his own problems came back, convulsing him with pain and the horrible fact of being sick.

Later on Charlie found himself shuddering from cold. The sun had slid away behind a mountain and the air came down cold from the snows again.

There was no way of being dry, or covered. It would be easier not to know anything, Charlie thought. Why do I only remember school and the last time I was ill in a comfortable bed under a roof? I am dying, he thought, and felt cold no more.

But he woke from that dream hearing sharks in the water, splashing and growling, speaking unknown words.

"Mama." said Elisabeth in a small croaking whisper.

The shark went away, and that was over. Not long afterwards there was smoke in the air. At first Charlie thought it was the smell of more sickness, but immediately the *moki* grounded on rock, stopping with a sudden jar, tipping itself out of the horizontal, pulling the pain in another direction.

Elisabeth was being taken away, clinging to what carried her. Charlie could do nothing about it. He did not look.

Wiremu was beginning to stand up. He did not seek to protect Charlie when something came for him and lifted him from the wet deck. Charlie was carried out of the *moki*, and Wiremu followed on his own two feet, and sometimes a hand to help him along the ground.

There was fire, Charlie found, and there was Elisabeth leaning on the Koroua, and still calling peevishly for Mama. The Koroua was not offended. He patted Elisabeth's shoulder and put wood on his fire.

Charlie lay where he was, warmer than he had been, the fire burning into his eyes until he closed them. He was sick again where he lay, the pain stiffening his muscles in and out of cramps.

Wiremu sat by the fire, feeling the same pains. Now and then he would walk away, sometimes on two legs, sometimes on three, like an animal. He would come back weakly, and sit down again, but never let himself lie down.

The Koroua was doing something horrible, the other side of the fire. Charlie knew he was understanding and not understanding at the same time, but he had two ideas going together. The Koroua was eating. He was eating meat on its bone. Charlie knew it was the leg of pig from the fire, but he knew at the same time that it was Elisabeth's leg, that the Koroua was quietly eating her over there, not caring who knew.

Charlie had long dreams about that, dreams that began when he was awake, stayed all the time he slept so that he could see himself asleep, and then continued after he woke.

There was cold water in his hot face, something between him and the fire that sprawled like a pair of tigers on the edge of the water, giving off a ferocity of heat that would tear to pieces anyone who came too close or teased the flames.

The Koroua was giving him water to drink, a sip at a time, and was washing his face with a cloth, no, with some mossy stuff soft as tiny feathers, complete with a stalky scrapiness.

The water went down cold, then bubbled up warm into his mouth again. Charlie clenched his teeth and swallowed it again. A little later he drank more. Something inside himself kicked at it, but let it stay.

Wiremu was drinking water then holding his mouth closed with his hands, forbidding anything to escape.

Elisabeth was sitting up, dipping her hand in a wooden basin of water and sipping it slowly.

"Mama came in the night," she whispered. "In her nightie like she does. She put a towel on my pillow." She had both her legs in front of her. Charlie knew that was right and wrong.

There was sunshine on his back and fire at his front. They were all in a clear place among trees. The water was lower down the slope, and there was no smell of rotting fish. There were other smells, but Elisabeth could not help that; but Charlie himself was ashamed at what happened close to himself. Wiremu had always walked off into the bushes when the sickness came upon him.

The Koroua went away. Charlie sat by the fire all day, and Elisabeth slept. Wiremu fetched wood. The Koroua had talked mostly to him in sign language, mooing and waving his arms and pointing to the sun.

"Gone to the cave," said Wiremu, but Charlie was feeling great surges of new discomfort then and could not speak.

The Koroua came back at the beginning of night. He had been to the cave and milked the sheep. He brought the milk with him, in the wooden bowl. Some had been spilt, but there was a long drink for each of them. Charlie's stayed down. Elisabeth lost a mouthful of curds, then held her breath and kept the rest.

The next day was overcast and a wind blew along the water. Charlie was sitting up now, taking little walks, and looking at things. He had a feeling now of always being here, of always having this family and no other. But the only way to make anywhere feel like home was to remember the real one. He looked around him and longed always to feel better than yesterday, to be at home in Jade Bay without losing the adventure of being with the Koroua. Just me and Wiremu, he thought. Elisabeth can stay at home and never come fishing again.

That night the Koroua did not return. There was nothing to eat. Charlie did not feel like eating much, but the feeling of food was quite a good one. They drank water instead of dining, and that was enough to sleep on. They drew closer to the fire and kept it smaller, like a home cat, not the lounging tigers the Koroua had created.

In the morning Elisabeth went down to the beach, picked her way through the last lingering fish, and went into the cold water. She wore the water while she washed her clothes, then wore them to the fire again.

"Last time it was salty water," she said. "Now it is river water."

"It is a lake," said Wiremu. "It must be, or the tides would come. I do not know how we can be by a lake, but I have thought about it. I do not think we can sail to the sea. But we can go down the lake to the end, and follow the river to Jade Bay."

Before they finished thinking about that they heard voices coming. Once again it was the calling of sheep. The Koroua had been to the cave and brought his flock with him.

Charlie looked at the animals, then at the ship, slowly putting two ideas together in the same nonsense way as when he thought Elisabeth was being eaten by the Koroua.

"I shall be Mrs Noah," said Elisabeth, having the same idea and not hesitating at all. "These are my lambs."

12

The Koroua seemed to have brought not only his sheep, which were in a nasty tangle and bad temper. He had bundled up all the property he could carry, bowls and roots, spoons, forks, wool, plates, cheeses like dumplings, and coils of plaited rope.

He gave the tangle of sheep to Wiremu and Charlie. Elisabeth came to greet her favourites in the flock.

"Where is the one with the black nose?" she asked the Koroua, when she had made her inspection.

The Koroua held up the knife to show her, then laid it down. He joined his bundle of fire to the one in that place. He put down ropes, bundles, cheeses, then the cups, and the glass and the tankard taken from his friend's grave.

He was ready to turn back and fetch more things. But as he turned to go his damaged legs stumbled under him, and he held the ground to keep himself up. His legs hurt, it was clear, because he had walked so far in the last few days.

Elisabeth filled his tankard at the spring nearby. There was always water, just as there was always fire, at the Koroua's camps. She took it to him, careful not to spill a drop, though that would not matter. She was busy being in her own house and not damping the mats.

Charlie thought she was pale and washed out, and that the Koroua was white under his weathered skin. He felt the bones of his own face and wondered how he looked. Wiremu had somehow dried up and become thin and bony.

The Koroua sipped his water, shaking his head, wondering about something. He muttered a word.

"It's his knee," said Elisabeth.

Charlie thought, without knowing why, of his grandfather, and that the Koroua, who was of course much older, had perhaps said that nobody had brought him a drink before.

The Koroua drank, then got up, and came to sit by the fire, leaning on a rock. He stretched his legs as well as he could, closed his eyes, and went to sleep.

Charlie and Wiremu tied the sheep up, then milked them. There was more milk than usual, and they made it a meal. It rested gently inside, and made them sleepy too.

"I will go back the way he came," said Wiremu. "He has left a lamb on the way, and that is what he was going for. You look after him and Itapeta, and I will follow the track. I know it, and it will be easy to see."

That was sense, because Wiremu could follow a track very much better than Charlie. Wiremu had once said Charlie needed posts and rails either side before he could see a trail.

Wiremu was still away when the Koroua woke

up, ready to go back himself. Charlie was able to explain what Wiremu was doing. The Koroua was still weary, and glad to sit for longer. Before long he got up and began to collect wood, and talk to the sheep.

Wiremu called to them from a long way off. He had found more than a lamb to carry. There were leather bags that had once been sheep, holding more of the Koroua's things, packed and sewn up like cushions. There was his digging stick, and pieces of polished wood tied in a bundle.

There was also a green thing on a string, carved from the green stone the Maoris used for all their jewels.

"He has met my people," said Wiremu. "It is a *tiki*. It is good luck, and many children."

"I have one at home," said Elisabeth. "I shall have eight children, five boys and five girls."

The Koroua could not tell them where he had got the *tiki*. It was a long time ago, he made them understand, before anything had happened to his legs. The Maoris had given it to him, and he had not seen them again.

"He does not know anything," said Wiremu.

It was long ago, the Koroua indicated. Then he skinned the lamb and set it to roast. The pig had been no good, he told them, grunting so that they understood. It had been made poisonous by eating dead fish, and that had made them ill.

The lamb was good. There were plates to eat it from, and roots cooked in ashes, ready to be eaten cold the next morning with new milk.

Then the Koroua packed up. They were moving, he said, going away. He had finished with the cave, with the lake. He could not find the way out by himself, and he could not manage to keep them. They would have to take him home with them. He said the name of the place, but they did not know it.

"We live somewhere else," said Charlie. "Jade Bay."

The Koroua could not get it right. He went on packing up, his most precious luggage the fire. And, as usual, he left one to smoulder at the place they left, taking only a small copy or model in twigs. He trusted no one else to do it.

"We aren't getting the treasure," said Charlie. "We didn't even get to the ship again."

"We'll find our way back," said Wiremu. "I can."

They went on beside the lake. There were dead fish all the way. The Koroua pointed out to them several times that it was their doing, but they could not tell why. If it was because the sea brought them there, then it was not their fault. It would have done it without them.

They went along easily, to stay with the Koroua and the sheep. During the journey one lamb broke its rope, and frisked about, without going far away. It was so used to being handled that Elisabeth could catch it at any time.

The lake came to an end round a corner. At one moment there was a great width of it, and all at once it shrank to a river.

The river went along gently, no more busy than the lake at first. Then the middle of it grew white where rocks began. Soon after that there was a distant drumming they could hear with their ears and feel with their feet.

"It's more sea," said Charlie.

"*Waitaka*," said Wiremu. "*Wata poro*." He was saying Waterfall in his own language, and then in Charlie's.

They soon saw it. The mountains ahead closed in on either side until there was no path to walk on, nowhere to go. Only the river moved on down hill in a rushing torrent, filling all the space, like a great moving plait, strands of itself being turned by rock and meeting again, arching over, turning to spray, and tumbling down, always the same, always different.

And as far as they could see along it the river was the same, heaving like a great lizard in a cart rut. It might have been a snake, but there are no snakes in those islands.

Down below, said the Koroua, the river is flat again. Before his legs were hurt he had been there. Down there he had been given the tiki. Somewhere beyond that again was the place he wanted to return to.

"*Poneke*," said Wiremu, his word for Wellington, beyond the strait. But that was not where the Koroua meant. In fact it seemed that he wanted to go to a place that was not there, and no one understood what he meant.

They understood what the river told them. There was no way down this valley to any place, whether it was there or not.

"Do we go back?" asked Charlie. "Now we've come all this way?"

"Yes," said Elisabeth, tired with travelling,

bored by walking all day, though she was the only one with shoes.

The Koroua knew what he was doing. He had known all the time that they could not follow the river, and he had not intended to. He wanted to go now into places he could not enter by himself. He would need help, they would need help, and perhaps only the sheep could manage, although they did not know the way at all.

The way was straight up the side of the mountain, and down the other side. He pointed into the high afternoon sun that came through the trees, up a slope that was nearly upright, where trees could not grow everywhere because of little stretches of true cliff like walls, and jutting-out crags like church roofs upside down.

If they went slowly it was not hard. It was up, up, up, with every step. But they had the sheep to lead first, and tie to a tree higher up, before coming down again to help the Koroua. He tried his best all the time, but steep climbs uphill were something he could not do, even using both arms.

His walking caused him pain with every step, or half step. He could only shuffle on this ground. If it was very rough as well as steep the roughness had to be taken away.

It took him four times as long as the rest of them to cover a distance, and it cost him four times as much work. He had to rest at the end of each section, so that altogether it took him five or six times as long. At those times everyone needed a rest.

"If we're getting home," said Charlie, "why

110

bother with the sheep? They are very small and poor."

"We shall have to eat them," said Wiremu. "One by one. We do not know how many days we shall be going."

When the light began to go, and there was a trickle of water near, the Koroua lit his fire from the embers he carried. There was cold lamb to eat, and cold cooked root. A long way below them the river boiled in its chasm. High above the stars looked out, the smoke of the fire smudging them.

They fell asleep on a wide ledge. Only the sheep called because there was not much to eat.

In the morning they went on again. Wiremu took the knife and marked the trees as they passed. "If we come back we know where we go," he said.

"We shan't come back," said Charlie. "This will take us home." He felt it had to, that it must, that only an extreme cruelty of events could bring anything else.

"We don't know," said Wiremu. "We got here, so we can't be lucky."

The mountain began to grow out of its trees. Parts of it were towering up as bare rock, like teeth, hard and rough. Elisabeth could not climb it. A Koroua like theirs never could. They had to find ways round and through, up narrow places between outcrops, where there was some sort of soil lying to make a place that held feet.

There were other problems. When the sun came out the snow higher up began to shift. There would be a whistling sliding noise, scraping as it came, and a block of snow like a door, or like a house, would come down solid and burst, and

111

settle solid again. There was nothing to be done about such falls, except be lucky enough to keep out of their way.

"Not us," said Wiremu.

"Us," said Charlie.

They went wearily back from tethering the sheep to a tree, carried up the luggage belonging to the Koroua, and then went down again to help him along. Wiremu was to one side, Charlie to the other, and Elisabeth pushed from the back.

Always, however he felt, and even though he was the weariest always, the Koroua pointed them upwards. It was the only way, he insisted.

At the end of that day he fell forward on his face and slept. Wiremu took the fire and lit a larger one. They ate the last of the lamb and cooked one root to eat between them, and that was all. They filled the tankard with snow and set it near the fire to melt. The sheep refused to give much milk, and the night fell cold and dispiriting over them.

The next day they rested. Charlie was sure this was all in vain. His hope of suddenly coming to a right place was vanishing moment by moment. Each time he guided the Koroua's foot to a foot-hold, each time he heaved with his shoulder, he thought how useless their work was.

"I always think that," said Wiremu. "I am more happy."

Charlie was too weary, too fed up, to argue at all. At that time he wanted to be away from all the people with him, to be alone at home, busy with something at the back of the house while the world went by at the front. Here there was no world to go by; he had to make it all.

They did not move the next day. They fed the sheep, but there was not much they would eat. The Koroua rested his limbs, and felt better. About the middle of the day he felt like smiling. He got out a cheese for them to eat, a quarter each, cut with the knife.

He went off slowly by himself with the knife and came back with supper, a lamb skinned and ready over his shoulders.

In the end, thought Charlie, feeling better after a hot meal, in the dusk under the trees, on some quite soft earth, in the end we shall eat all the sheep and he will start on us. That is all that will happen. But he did not believe it. There was some hope of something.

In the middle of the next day the hope went away. It began to rain, and sometimes the rain was hail, and now and then snow. The only warm place then was right in among the sheep, using their wool to keep warm; and the sheep preferred to huddle together.

After the snow had fallen they walked through it up the final slope of the ridge to its top. Charlie hoped to see something, a city, people, Jade Bay. But in the high mist there was only a steep slope down, and beyond the bottom of the steep slope another hillside going up, with the feeling that it was so for ever and ever, into the hazy distance.

The sun stabbed through the trees and made them steam more mist into the saturated air, and drops of pure new rain fell from the air round them.

Long afterwards the Koroua was up there with them, though they told him they had come nowhere. He said nothing they understood, after looking and seeing what they saw. But they felt that he meant to go down again, that this way had disappointed him and dashed his hopes.

They went down a little way and lit the fire, sitting by it into the dark. Elisabeth wandered away to talk to sheep. Suddenly she was calling out, calling for Charlie, for Wiremu, in a voice that was filled with unknown excitement, or panic.

13

Elisabeth's voice came without words at first, a shriek that might be fear, or might be joyful excitement. Charlie thought she had fallen off something.

Her words became clearer. *"Whakatata mai,"* she was calling. In fact she was giving orders, "Come to this place".

Charlie came. Now he was sure something had happened to a sheep. There was no time to count them, but he looked that way when he thought of them, and stumbled. Wiremu, watching the ground in the dark, was ahead of him, calling back in Maori to Elisabeth. She shouted back, but did not understand all his words. Nor did Charlie. When he and Wiremu talked they used a sort of mixed language, where Charlie thought in English and Wiremu thought in Maori.

Wiremu got there first and began shouting in turn. He had seen something, that was all. Elisabeth had seen something too, and that was a lot less.

Then Charlie, coming up the last slope to the edge of the ridge, saw it too. There is only one thing you see perfectly at night, and there it was.

115

A light shone somewhere below them, a long way down the next valley.

"It's a star," said Charlie. There were stars above, but a star might be below them if they were high enough up. Or it seemed possible to Charlie.

"It is our light at the store," said Elisabeth. "It is just as bright."

Charlie's insides turned over and his heart flapped in his chest. For a moment it seemed that dreadful illness was coming over him again. Then it wasn't so. He merely felt that all they had to do was walk in that direction, and everything would come right, that Mama and Papa would come running to meet them, that Wiremu's dog would leap round them; that he would no longer have responsibility for Liss, and Mama could take her over again.

Wiremu was talking to himself, trying to explain words he had not got in a language he did not quite know. He was feeling the ground for stones, for rocks, for something he could put in a certain place so that he knew the place again.

Later on, when things were not as he left them, he told Charlie what he meant to do. He meant to place a line of stones pointing to the light. The stones would be visible by day, and by looking in the direction they indicated, then Jade Bay might be visible. You might have to look very hard.

But for now he was too excited to explain. He pulled at stones, moving some, not being able to move others, and told Charlie to stand where he was while he lined things up.

Elisabeth joined in at first, then stopped. "It's

silly," she said. "We aren't going to stay here. We're going there."

"Not in the dark," said Wiremu.

Down among the trees by the fire the Koroua called, "Hoo, hoo," his way of ordering them back.

"It is a light," Charlie shouted. "It is Jade Bay."

The Koroua could not walk up here alone in the dark. Instead he made a brighter star for them to come back to, opening up the fire and throwing on resinous branches.

That night of all, with hope ahead, the smoke rich in the trees, was the one Charlie remembered for ever; and he knew it at the time.

"They've gone to bed," said Elisabeth suddenly. She was right – down in Jade Bay the light went out, and there was nothing but darkness on the land. Overhead the stars were strained out of view by the filter of mist. No star had been so bright as the lamp of home.

The Koroua was pleased to hear what they explained. He understood that they had seen a fire, because that was the only light they had. It was difficult trying to explain a point of light like a star, because he thought they were being foolish about a star, not wise about getting home.

In the morning Wiremu was very angry, and spent some time sulking. He and Charlie had seen to the sheep the very first thing, leaving Elisabeth to play about, helping herself to meat from the cooked lamb, fetching water for the Koroua, who was stiff and slow in the mornings, or talking to Treasure. She slipped away up the hillside to look for the light again.

"It won't be there," said Charlie, and Wiremu

had something to say too, but lost it when a sheep began to skip about for some reason of its own.

Later on, though, both of them went up to the top to look in the right place as carefully as they could.

"We'll have to guess," said Charlie, on the way.

"No," said Wiremu. "We shall know."

They did not know. Elisabeth had decided the place was untidy, and had put all Wiremu's pointing stones into one heap, and smoothed out the footprints. That was when Wiremu became angry and walked off alone, and would help no one do anything all the morning.

But since he had eaten nothing, and no one took him anything because he might be in the mood for killing and eating pakehas with stupid families, he gradually found his way back.

"We shall wait another day," he said. "And see the light again. There have been wars among our people for moving stones. It must never be done."

"It was a mess," said Elisabeth. But she was sorry, all the same, and brought Wiremu water in her pretty glass.

After that they took the Koroua up to the top of the slope so that he too could see what there was.

Until the sun was well up, there was nothing to see but the straggles of mist among the trees. But the shapes, like curtains, went further and further away and the country became more clear.

"It's still hazy," said Charlie, squinting into the distance. "I can't see any houses."

It gradually became certain that the mist had truly gone, and that the flat part far away was the sea. The new valley they were in now, and where the sheep were tied, led out to some lower land, covered with trees, and the sea was beyond that.

Jade Bay was on the edge of the sea, down in flat land.

"If we lit a big fire," said Charlie, "they would see it and come for us."

"They would think it was the Koroua," said Wiremu. "They would ask my people, and my people at the pa would tell them about the Koroua."

"The Koroua is all right," said Elisabeth, stroking his hand. "He is my big brother."

"That is not what they say," said Wiremu.

The Koroua was not interested in any more talk about what might be or might not be. If there had been a light of any sort, even a fallen star, then that was where they would go. It also seemed that he had not caught sight of the sea since he came here, and wanted to get to it at once.

"He was born here," said Wiremu. "He did not come. He cannot walk, so his mother and father brought him."

"He will tell them we have been nice to him," said Elisabeth, patting the Koroua again to make certain. "We shall get biscuits."

They were ready to go. They had their whole camp with them, and left nothing but a fire that would go out on its own only after a long time. They took seeds for a new one, and set off.

The Koroua was no better at going down the hillsides. He slipped and slithered and fell on his back. He had been determined before, but now he would not stop; he would not give in at all. They went as fast as he could move for two long days, until everyone was overtired and there was nothing solid to eat. In the morning, when they had all slept badly, Elisabeth saw that the Koroua's feet had been bleeding, and said her patient could not walk until he was better.

"We are nearly there," said Wiremu, though in fact they were merely following the valley down, with the crags growing steep and steeper above them. Probably what had tired them most the day before was a place where a huge piece of mountain had broken from the top and crashed its way down into the valley, tearing away all the trees, blocking the valley itself and making a lake, and being impossible to cross. They had had to walk back up the side of the lake, cross the fierce river, and go down the other side. The track of the rock fall was as wide as a town, and strewn with boulders the size of houses, with now and then a Town Hall or a Cathedral tipped among the wreckage.

That day was a rest. There was even grass for the sheep beside the water in a natural meadow.

"We follow the river," said Wiremu, after consulting the Koroua. "When it gets to the sea we follow the coast, and then we shall come to Jade Bay. It is simple."

There was not much else they could do. Wiremu's pointing stones would have had to stay on the ridge, and there was no way of telling whether they were on the right line. They had to go with the country, because that was the only place there was.

"I knew it didn't matter," said Elisabeth, reminded of the stones, not wanting to be blamed

120

by Mama when they got home; or when they probably didn't.

"You didn't know it then," said Charlie. "Play with your doll."

The Koroua killed another lamb. It made the flock more manageable. The Koroua was more and more tired. He would not give up, but his legs stopped working if he walked too far. Then he had to stop and rub them, to be rid of the cramp. The distorted muscles could be seen fighting under the skin, and sweat would run on the Koroua's face.

They took another day's rest. After that the land grew flatter, but there were more tangles under the trees. There were marshes to walk round. One whole day they walked about a small hill, starting with it over to the right, beyond the river. They followed the water, and the hill was on the left for far too long. They ended that day with the hill on the right again, and just looking as it had in the morning, as if they had come nowhere.

And Elisabeth was crying because Treasure had been left behind. She put him to bed last night, she said, and forgot him this morning.

Charlie drew a map on the sand of a small river beach. "That is the hill," he said. "We walked in a circle beside the river. This is the river. It comes right round nearly to itself again in a big winding."

"I remember those trees," said Wiremu. "I counted the pines, and there were nine in the clump. I went there in the night for a *pipi*, I am sure."

Charlie went with him to look, a hundred yards away. Wiremu did not know which tree, but it was one of nine. And a hundred yards beyond again was their fire of last night. Beside it, under a cover-

121

let of stone, was Treasure, abandoned but loved and wanted.

They spent a second night in the same camp, the nights separated by a day's wasted walking. Elisabeth knew it was a miracle of some sort, because of finding Treasure. The Koroua looked at Charlie's map, stumped to the old camp, laughed rather sadly, and went to sleep chuckling and shaking his head. We won't tell anyone, said the chuckles and the shake.

I think it is the South Pole, Charlie said to himself. All the places join together with black lines. But there were no black lines on the ground. He caught fish, small and black, with his steel hook. The Koroua's bone hook caught a large and silver one that was ready to bite while it was being cooked.

The next day he and Wiremu went ahead. "To see the lie of the land," Charlie said. "It does not speak the truth."

They were able to go from loop to loop of the river, instead of following its idle wanderings. "It's following a black line," Charlie told Wiremu. "They're straight."

In the quiet of one night something sang to them. The river fattened and gurgled and changed its smell. They had to shift the fire away from its sandy edge. And beyond that quiet tide rising there was the shuffle of distant waves on a beach, licking and falling back, rising and falling, the sound travelling up the river in the stillness of night.

A day later the river straightened itself. The far bank drew further away. The ground grew sandy, and the sheep were very miserable about the salty scrub that grew there.

The sheep could be let loose when they got to the town, said the Koroua. They thought now he was saying Jade Bay, but in a very difficult way. It does not matter, thought Charlie. That is where it will be.

Gradually during one day, when they all went quite well because the Koroua walked on his own over sand, they began to wonder whether the river was still beside them, or had turned to sea as they came along it.

"There should be boats," said Charlie. "They'll be round the corner, of course."

"The divers might be out," said Wiremu.

"It does not feel like home," said Elisabeth. "We have walked to nowhere. I do not like nowhere. The sand is stinging my face."

14

The tide came nudging up the river again, pushing with waves that thinned out as they spread. What was man-high at first was doll-high over the wave before it, but the whole tide lifted itself in steps, riding over the river water.

It was sad, sad, sad, during a long afternoon to see the water coming in and then going out. Both Charlie and Wiremu felt that they had come as far as they could, and found it not worth the trouble. They were as far from home as they had been, and here nothing shone any light. There was nothing here in the sand, beyond the trees at the forest edge.

The Koroua rested and thought about things. ''Hoo,'' he said at last, and stood up, gathering up what he carried. There was further to go, he told them.

The further to go was only along the sea shore. A buffeting wind was coming in over the waves, the tide was up, sand flew and stung, and occasional wave-tops were launched into the air and dropped a sticky wetness on them. The sand underfoot sank and slid under their weary feet all the way.

"I was going home," said Elisabeth, bravely. "But I didn't."

The Koroua signalled them to keep moving, to follow him. The sheep hated this place and complained all the time. Sand disgusted them.

Elisabeth trailed behind and stopped being brave. Charlie went back to her and gave her a lamb to pull. He thought she would be happier if she could be cross with something.

They toiled a long way. The forest went further back inland, and the coast went round to meet it.

"It's another of those loops," said Charlie. "We'll get even more nowhere if we don't look out."

The Koroua stopped walking. He was ahead of them, and turned to beckon them on, turning forward again very often, as if they were playing Grandmother's Footsteps, and looking back to them again.

He was more interested in what was ahead, or perhaps in what he thought was ahead. He was looking hard and trying to bring something into existence, to remember something, perhaps.

There was nothing to see but a tree stump, Charlie thought. But on a second look it was not a tree stump caused by nature, or perhaps not a tree stump at all. If he wanted, Charlie could think it was a thick post upright in the ground, because of the way the top was square, and the sides were flat.

Wiremu went up to it, pulled something from it, and brought that thing back. It was an iron nail, bent and rusted, but real; bent by being hammered in, rusted from long years of sea and rain.

125

It had held something to the post. Charlie found that thing. It was an oblong of wood, bent and gappy from age, but once a new sign of some sort, painted on both sides. One side was plain, or the words had gone utterly.

The other side could just be read. "J," said Charlie, holding the board the way up that made the best sense. "Jack. No, that's not it. It's JAB. No, JAD, Jad. JADB. No. JADE, JADE BAY. Which way was it pointing?" He thought it was a direction sign, and that the post was a sign-post to tell people where to go. There was only one actually in Jade Bay, and it pointed the way to the river, as if people did not already know. There was no road to anywhere else, not even one at the river pointing to Jade Bay. So it was very strange to have a sign here to tell someone how to get there, out in the middle of nowhere.

The Koroua thought something different. He said some things quite quickly, and walked on, as fast as he could.

"Hey," said Wiremu, "this is a road, eh? Look, a Koroua could follow it, even a pakeha." The Koroua looked round and nodded, recognizing the name they used for him.

"How so?" asked Charlie. "It's like everywhere."

"Well I'm wrong," said Wiremu. "I thought you could follow a track if it had a fence each side of it, but I am wrong. You can't even see the fences."

Charlie saw them after a hard look. Wiremu was right. They were on a road, even if trees grew in the middle of it, and on either side were the remains of garden fences.

In a while there were the remains of houses, not only fallen in from age but turned and twisted, sometimes even lifted and tipped on their sides. No one could tell what colour they had been painted, because there was only the bare wood now; and the corrugated iron sheets of the roofs were red, red, red, with rust, or gaping with holes.

"I think this is Jade Bay," said Wiremu, coming to a stop, than wandering along slowly. "We are getting to the middle."

"But what has happened?" said Charlie. "It is wrong."

It was wrong. He was about to explain that this was another place altogether when he came to an absolute stop, and stood. A shiver went across his shoulders, down his back, crawled behind his knees, tickled his heels and his toes, then climbed across his kneecaps, across his stomach, and ran up into his face. He felt himself blush. He again had a severe pain in his back and could hardly stand.

In front of him was a ghost, but an impossible one. There was the store, where Papa bought and sold goods, with its front verandah, the side verandahs, the steps, the store window, the parlour window, and across the front, over the steps, the name, C Snelling. His own name, his father's name.

But this sign was loose at one end; the paint had almost gone; the store itself had settled to one side; there was dried mud covering one side of the steps and smoothing the square ends of the other; the windows were broken or missing, the door hung ajar. There was no Papa near, no Mama tidying up; there was no smoke at the chimney. This was home, but a long-dead one.

The Koroua grinned. He was not surprised. He did not mind that a tree was now growing out through the roof. He seemed to think it was amusing in some way, though not in a funny one. He threw up his hands, meaning, "What else can you expect?" and went to the steps. He had difficulty going up them, but would accept no help. He went up, crossed the verandah to the dangling door, testing each inch of his way, and peered in.

He shouted into the building. There was no reply. He thought this was a further sort of joke, and came down the steps once more.

"The tree is in my bedroom," said Elisabeth. "Papa will cut it down."

"No," said Charlie, "something has happened. This is all wrong. We have got back too far in front, and everything has fallen in."

"There is no pa," said Wiremu, who had been looking for the way to his village, part of the town really. "They have all gone away."

"I will go to school," said Elisabeth. "There are my friends."

There were no friends. There was no school. There was only the plan of it, where short pillars of brick had held the building off the wet ground, four across the ends, eight along the sides, and other footings for the verandah.

"This is another place," said Wiremu.

The Koroua did not seem to think so. He went into the outline of the school, chose his desk, and stood there. With a look of mischief he put up his hand to give an answer, and laughed loudly.

Just across the road should have been the church. Now there was a heap of crumbled wood, with the one stone wall that held the bell still standing. There was no bell.

The Koroua was solemn now. He hunted about round the building until he found a small stone showing. He began to dig by it, finding writing on it, tracing the words with his fingers.

Charlie went to help. The Koroua was no longer laughing, but he was not altogether sad, digging out a headstone in the churchyard. This, he explained to Charlie, will make everything clear, and he waved to everything, as if that did it.

Oh God, thought Charlie, having a prayer. It is my own tomb. This is what Korouas know. He has not eaten us in a way we understand, but he has taken away all we know, and now he is telling me. Please do not let him tell Liss.

However, the name chiselled into the stone was not his own. It was one that did not surprise him completely. It read LUDWIG WEBBER, and below it was the date and some places. The first date was 1781, and the place JADE BAI, and the second was 1842, and the place JADE BAY. The two places were not quite the same, and the dates were very long ago. Charlie knew perfectly well that the first date was before New Zealand was known at all, and that the second was early in the pakeha times, oh fifty years ago, before civilization, before the telegraph, before Miss MacDonald and the South Pole.

Wiremu came to look. "Why is he digging them up?" he asked. "That's a bad thing to do. That person can't have been born here, because it wasn't here then. There was only our pa, and I can't find that. What has happened, Charlie?"

Charlie could not tell him. Here was Jade Bay, somehow as the Koroua had known it, somehow as Charlie knew it, but for both of them much had changed. Charlie was very worried by it, but the Koroua seemed glad to find anything. It is the earthquake, Charlie wanted to say, the earthquake came here when we were somewhere else. They are all . . . The next thought would not come; and Wiremu was talking about something else.

"You want to see this, then," Wiremu said, because he had found something the other side of the church. "This one they never got buried. It must have been a flying one."

The flying one was made of bones. They all knew what it was, because the skeletons of whales littered the coast, often going bad like the fish on the lake shore, but the badness lasting for months instead of a few days. This skeleton now lay like the timbers of a strange building next to the timbers of the church, the carpenter having gone mad with bending tools.

Elisabeth gazed into an eye-socket as big as herself. "If I went to sleep in there would it dream?" she asked.

No one knew. For the time being they tied the restless sheep to the great bones of the whale and let them crop the churchyard weeds. The Koroua, like Elisabeth, looked at the skull, but he thought it too small to live in, and found a place between it and the church's stone wall. Here he laid down almost all his gear, and made them put most of theirs.

Charlie did not know what the Koroua intended. It was only another question without answers. What was this place? was the biggest question, and no one answered it. What had happened to it?

Charlie thought he had a throb of an idea, pulsing down his back, hurting him all over again, but he could not get hold of it. It was something beyond earthquake, but he could not bring it into his mind. It was as remote as some parts of the multiplication tables.

"If a place has died," said Wiremu, "died like a man, then we could visit its ghost. Would we die too?"

The Koroua was satisfied that he knew where he was. He led them out of the town by another road. There was no signpost, but the road took them to a river. It was not the river they had followed down but quite a different one. At its edge were the remains of buildings, and a little way upstream (the tide was now falling and they saw how the water flowed) the remains of a bridge showed on either bank.

The Koroua was satisfied with this state of affairs. He even began to sing a little song, not out loud, but to himself.

This isn't a Koroua, Charlie suddenly thought, looking at him again. This is . . . but he could only think that the Koroua must be something worse; or that Korouas were ghosts, that this was Ludwig Webber, died 1842, escaped from the churchyard and living wild in the forest. It is a Koroua, he decided.

The Koroua, or not, had brought Charlie's fishing line with him. He baited the sharp metal hook with a bob of fat from the last lamb, and bobbed it into the water, just exactly where he meant. He knew this river, he knew that a fish would be behind that stone, until it tasted the hook.

Then it was on the bank, and they all looked at supper.

There was wood in plenty for burning. The Koroua blew on his carried embers, added splinters to them, made a fire on a fallen headstone, and hung the fish to cook. There was fish. There was milk. There was the last cheese, so young it was not yet mouldy. Charlie went off by himself before it was dark and found what he knew would be there. It was very uncanny to go on to his own verandah, broken as it was by time he had never known, and pick fat bunches of the black Hamborough grapes he knew would be growing there, that had been growing the morning he left to go fishing on a low tide.

They are in some way imaginary, he thought. But they tasted better than anything had for a long time, and the stranger the sweeter, he fancied.

In the morning, he thought, everything will have come right. They were not expecting us, that is all. It will be put right, and Papa will be angry because of the grapes. And he cried a little, because that would be the sweetest thing of all. He went to sleep fiercely loving Papa, depending on him to be frowning there in the morning.

He was not. The Koroua was moving wood about, making a hut, far too small for all of them. It does not matter, Charlie said, almost aloud. I have my own house.

But in a little while the Koroua stopped work,

looked at them, turned them to face the way they had come into this town.

"Ship," he said, pointing the way to the mountains. "Ship," and pointed to the river, waving his arms to show a journey, meaning clearly that they had to return to the lake and bring the ship down the river, because this river was the one coming from the lake, down the gorge, and to this place.

Wiremu shook his head. "It will kill us," he said.

But the Koroua was quite clear about things. He was staying here. He had no strength left. He would die here if they did not bring the ship. If they all stayed they would all die. They could take three sheep, and any other thing, including the knife. But they had to leave now, while the way back was still clear.

15

Telling Charlie and Wiremu what they had to do Now took a long time, and Now turned into Then. The Koroua clearly said he could not manage another long journey, either with his legs or with his heart. Meanwhile Elisabeth had wandered away, not interested for long in all the arm-waving by the Koroua, or the sulky stubbornness of her brother and Wiremu.

She came back, and went away again. Charlie gradually realized that she had taken some fire with her. He did not think that was a good idea, because she might drop it anywhere, burning down the remains of Jade Bay, or stand on it, or even sit on it.

Papa said sometimes that sitting on the fire was the cure for toothache, but that was a joke. Charlie thought he should see what Elisabeth was doing, and went looking and calling, "Liss, Liss."

She came running to meet him, carrying something under one arm, and a spiky thing in the other.

"Put it back," said Charlie, knowing what she had done. Then he stopped, because it was impossible. What she had could not be found here.

He turned right round and looked back along the empty and tumble-down street.

The store belonging to C Snelling was still a misshapen ruin.

But Elisabeth was carrying a large tin of pork and beans under her arm, and the tin-opener in the other. Cases of these tins were always stacked in the store; but how was this one here?

"I can't get it open," Elisabeth was saying. "I'm making the dinner. I lit the fire, and we can have one each."

In a back garden, where not many trees grew, and the house had fallen in on itself, there was a large burnt piece of ground littered with black branches. In the middle of it there was a tiny fire, fit for the doll that sat beside it. The four plates, with spoons on them, sat round the fire with the doll. Beside each plate there was a large tin of pork and beans, shiny new, with clean labels.

"There's a lot more," said Elisabeth, showing him a wooden box with eight more tins in it. There was a label on the box. It had C Snelling Jade Bay written on it in blue ink, with not a smudge, not a dusty mark, new as any label that came into the store from a delivery ship.

Charlie had to sit down to think about things. If this place was Jade Bay why were the tins out here and not in the store? If this was not Jade Bay, then why were the tins here at all?

"It just looks like them," he told Elisabeth in the end. "But we'll find it's something else, because it can't be true."

The Koroua came along then with Wiremu, being still in the middle of telling all three of them what to do. The tins meant nothing to him, and he did not understand the labels.

But he could read Ludwig, Charlie remembered. I don't know what he is.

Wiremu had no difficulty with the tin. Charlie did not know whether he could read, but he knew how to dig the spike of the tin-opener into the top of the tin, and then how to claw and saw his way round the top with the hook. He lifted the lid right off and licked it.

The Koroua was astonished. He smelt the pork and beans. He dipped a finger in and tasted. He scooped some out and ate it.

"Share it out," said Charlie, because the pork and beans were real enough. As for other things, while they ate the pork and beans cold round the dolls' fire, he rather thought that this Jade Bay was a sort of vision or memory left by people from the real Jade Bay who had visited here very recently, a camp like home, but built to grow old at once. Yet nothing made sense.

"Don't think about it, Tiari," said Wiremu, spooning a last gravy from the can. "We'd better do what he says."

The Koroua was pleased with the empty can. It would carry water, or fire, or milk, he indicated. It could be a kettle for making tea. But he shrugged his shoulders because there was no tea.

They all agreed that this fire was the light they had seen, and that it had been lit for them and been very large.

"Up there," said Wiremu, looking through trees to the hunch-backed ridges of mountain and the snows beyond. "That's where we were." He

136

thought he knew where they had stood to see the light. Charlie thought he was wishing only.

In the wooden box of tins, where it must have fallen, Charlie found a scrap of paper. It was Siggy's telegraph paper, yellow and official. It had MESSAGE RECEIVED printed on one side, but no writing. On the back of it someone had written numbers and dates, but there was no meaning to them. Wiremu looked at them, and handed the paper to the Koroua.

The Koroua looked at them slowly, then sharply, then was pointing to the last two figures of the date, asking, asking, whether they were right, whether they meant the year they were not in. He began counting on his fingers.

"Yes," said Charlie. "That's this year." He thought it was a silly question. Everyone knew what year it was, except Liss, he explained. The Koroua did not listen, and Elisabeth went on stirring the empty tin with a stick, making a hot bath for Treasure. The Koroua went on counting to himself. Then he held up both hands for ten, and opened and closed them more times than Charlie could count. He thought it was about fifty, quite old even for a Koroua.

"A hundred," said Elisabeth. It was her best number. She was pleased with the Koroua for being it so tidily.

It was not long before the Koroua sent them away. He kept the tin-opener and most of the tins. Charlie and Wiremu carried one each, because Wiremu could open a tin with the knife, and often had.

They refused to take any sheep. "I hate them,"

said Charlie, and Wiremu agreed. Elisabeth said goodbye to a lamb, but it was thinking of something else entirely. The Koroua looked at the knife, and then thought he would live on beans. Of course he must always before have killed lambs without a knife.

He said he would build a large fire that night. All they had to do was bring the ship down the river, and it would come here. Once it was here they would repair it enough to sail somewhere else. The Koroua was clear about it but was unable to explain. He spluttered some words, and they had no meaning.

Before they went he made Elisabeth a comb. It was in case they met friends, he seemed to say. He saw them off, standing against a tree and waving as they went further and further off.

"We could cut across the corner," said Charlie. "Until we meet the river we came down."

But that was not a good idea. The clear ground was at the river edge, and further into the forest the undergrowth ate up all the light and they could not see where to go at all, or in what direction.

Elisabeth said, "I'm tired of all this walking. My feet hurt. I want to play in the houses. Then she was running back towards the town, and would not listen to them.

"She can do that," said Charlie, "and she can't walk."

"Let her go," said Wiremu. "We are quicker without her. Come on."

"Wait," said Charlie. "She might not get there."

In half an hour there was a shout from the town, the Koroua sending "Hoo, hoo," and Wiremu replying with a deep and chesty Maori cry the same words. There was a single "Hoo" from the town, and a single one from Wiremu.

"That's all right then," said Charlie, not being sure at all. "He doesn't want her," he said.

"Well," said Wiremu, "do we?"

They went on. They went on fast. They did two days' journey before dark. Then they lit a fire, but with some difficulty because there was only a tiny single spark left. The Koroua had always kept the flames himself, and Charlie had not taken the same care, had not paused often enough to feed with both wet and dry twigs the infant blaze.

Wiremu caught a fish at dusk. It was not very large, but they made do with it, not wanting to open the tins until they had to, though they were wearisome to carry.

At the end of the second day they camped by the loop in the river, where they had been twice already. The covered fire there was all black charcoal cinder, growing from their own coals into a scorching eye in the wind, too hot to cook by. They had two long river fish, and four small birds caught alive on the sticky shoots of a tree, a twiggy mouthful each.

The next day they passed the great landslide. In its upper reaches there were still stirrings and chattering falls of rock, and shiftings of its tongues.

The day after that they reached the ridge, the place where Wiremu's stones had been tidied by Elisabeth. They did not wait here to light a fire, because the day was not yet near dark. Instead they pushed on, before dark reaching the river

139

beyond, and its throat of rapids between the jaws of rock.

Between the rapids and the lake, in the calm dark river, pulled by the invisible current, the ship edged its heavy way along by itself. It had worked down the lake itself, and now was seeking its way out.

"We could have stayed there," said Wiremu. "It's on its way alone. How do we get on?"

"*Moki*," said Charlie.

The first *moki* was a failure. It was taken by the current before they could paddle or pole it across. They had to jump into the water and flounder to the shore.

"We could just walk back," said Wiremu. "If it's coming on its own. It'll never sail again. We'll go back and wait for it."

"Then the Koroua will get the treasure," said Charlie. "We don't want that to happen."

"No," said Wiremu. But he was not very interested in treasure. He was quite sure, he said, that the pakehas would get it, because they always did, so what was the point? He sat and plaited ropes. Since he was here he would help. He wanted to shoot through the rapids for the sake of doing it. So he plaited and plotted and planned.

Charlie thought the plan was right. They made another *moki*, well up the river, and let it float downstream, faster and faster, until they came up to the ship and could get alongside.

The first attempt was a failure, and they lost another *moki*. But the next time everything came right. The *moki* twirled itself round in an eddy behind the ship, hit it hard with one corner, tipped

140

itself up, and more or less threw Wiremu up on the broken rudder and let him climb aboard and make fast the rope attached to the *moki*.

Charlie followed more slowly, and let the *moki* drift away. It was tethered by the rope, and did not escape.

"You should have stayed on it," said Wiremu. "You are going back to land for the fire and the tins and for firewood. I will pull you aboard again. Hurry up."

Charlie obediently ferried himself across, collected the tins, bundled up firewood, stored some fire safely in a hollow log, and came back to the raft. He relied on Wiremu to know what he was doing with a ship and with a raft.

All these attempts and visits to the shore had used up the daylight, and shadows were falling across the water when Charlie got on the raft. He shouted for a pull, and Wiremu began to draw him across.

Because the *moki* was in slower water, and because Wiremu pulled the rope attached to it, and because Charlie was slow to remember to unfasten the rope end of the raft from a bush, the raft did not come easily. Wiremu had to pull hard, his feet against the bottom of the rail, his back arched tight. Also, for some reason, he had not started soon enough. Charlie thought he must have been looking round, checking the treasure.

At first nothing happened. Charlie was picking at the knot he had made, but disentangling plaited and knotted creeper is a job for slow times, not when your ship is beginning to dip towards a long water slide of the roughest kind.

The ship began to move out onto the swiftest current, and gave a lurch, feeling itself ready to go.

Wiremu sat down on the deck, still drawing in the raft as well as he could. Charlie felt the lurch too, down the stiff rope. He sat down, because the *moki* became excited.

The current flowing to the top of the rapids had taken the ship when it was pulled into the middle of the river. The *moki* began to follow it.

Charlie lay on his back and held the fire out of the water. The water overwhelmed the *moki* and then ran through between its logs, sluicing itself away. Charlie held the fire up high, and could do nothing with the other hand alone.

The *moki* was behind the ship now, being pulled by it. Wiremu was on the ship, holding on to the rope. Charlie was on the *moki*.

We should not have done this, he thought. But if Liss does not know she cannot tell.

There was a back-breaking thud, and the *moki* went down a sudden steep step. Charlie rolled off the edge and held on with one hand, the other bearing the irreplaceable fire for their next meal.

Wiremu was shouting for him and he could not hear over the noise of the water.

I shall drown, he thought. There is nothing I can do about it.

16

There was a sudden hot water in Charlie's hand, then nothing at all. The river had taken the seeds of fire away. Charlie used the empty hand to hold on to something, because that was all it would do, search and hold, and hold fast.

The thing he was holding held him too. If it was rope then it was tightening on his wrist, nipping. The harder Charlie held the harder it held, until he could hardly bear it. He felt that it was dragging him under water, pulling his face into the flow, and not allowing him to breathe.

The *moki* was under him still, and hitting rock. Each time it hit it came up and hit him in turn, but not so hard. The water that made the first hard hit softened the second, so that nothing broke.

There was a moment's rest while the *moki* swirled without striking. In that moment Charlie saw what held him so firmly. Wiremu was in the water with him, one hand holding the rope, the other holding Charlie. Wiremu was a swimmer, but in the tumble of the rapids he could do nothing. His eyes were watching, though, while Charlie thought his own were seeing nothing useful.

The ship was not in sight. He had time to pull

143

Wiremu nearer to the *moki*, but not to bring him aboard it. Charlie could not let go of it himself because its rope was wound round one arm. That was what held him out of the water long enough to breathe. Then he was under again, his head being pulled in one direction, and his arms in two more.

Wiremu was fighting the water, watching it, hitting out at it with the arm loosely in the rope. His lips were drawn back, and he was intent on winning.

There was cold darkness gathering round them both, and too much noise to be heard. There were swooping fountains from one side and then another, and long slitherings down gullets of rock, in a mixture of air and water that felt like treacle, dragging and clinging with its speed and pressure.

The speed took them through the rapids. The *moki* sheltered them from the worst blows. It was so heavily made of sappy wood that the water could not toss it aside and had to carry it like part of itself.

There was a singing in Charlie's ears, like silence, or some sort of deafness. Some of it was water, twitching against the eardrum. Some of it was the pulsing of water, but not taking his limbs and throwing them about, not battering him.

He was not moving. Or only his legs were swaying. His back, aching where it had ached before, was comfortable against a solid thing, and the legs floated in the river.

Something let go of one arm. Someone said a Maori word that Mama would have been cross about, or pretended she did not know. Charlie

144

disentangled his other arm from the creeper rope and dug his elbows into wet sand. He lifted himself up and looked round.

There was not much to see. Somewhere to one side were the white flickerings of falling water. He had to adjust his hearing to hear the rush and roar, because he had grown so used to them that they no longer got themselves heard. To the other side there was a long darkness with a brighter sky stretching into the distance, edged with beech trees, like most of The Knuckle.

"Ship goes on its own," said Wiremu. "Get there without you and me, Tiari." He was sitting up and shivering. Charlie sat right up and shivered.

"Are we alive?" he asked.

"No," said Wiremu. "This is one pakeha bad place. We came down into it."

"I drank most of it," said Charlie. "It isn't salt any more."

"*Tote* all washed out of lake now," said Wiremu.

"Liss," said Charlie, trying to remember. "Where's Liss?"

"Itabeta with Koroua," said Wiremu. "You brought fire, Tiari?"

Charlie spread his hands to show he had no fire any more. But he had to say so, because it was too dark for Wiremu to see. He knew already. He remembered Elisabeth turning back. He hoped she was all right. He hoped the Koroua was all right. He hoped the Koroua did not mind.

"We'll find the ship," said Wiremu. "Throw stones until we hear it. Listen for noise."

They threw stones, walking along the bank from the little cove where they had been washed up. In the end they saw the tilted hulk, listing over to one side, and nose down in a dismal attitude. It was wrecked again, or at least grounded, and they walked to the side. That turned out to be the bottom of it, the keelboards lying on a gravel bank, but still underwater. The way aboard was round the other side, riding on the *moki* again.

"Better on land," said Charlie. "We haven't anything to eat, we haven't any fire, we haven't anything."

"Huh," said Wiremu, thinking Charlie was wrong but not promising anything.

The ship was big enough to come through the rapids without getting wet all over. It had been heavy enough to ride fairly level, but not too much so. If it had been perfectly balanced as a ship should be it would have filled and sunk, because there were holes along one side. Pinnacles of sea-rock had made those holes, and held her fast since she sank.

Charlie wondered what the divers were doing, not knowing they would never find her.

Wiremu was feeling his way about. There were things in the way that had not been there before. Fallen pieces from the mast littered the sloping foredeck and tilted cabin roof. Girders from the cabin sides stuck out into the air, pointed, jagged, at all levels, especially ready for the eye. Other pieces crackled underfoot. They were dry firewood. Wiremu had thrown his bundle aboard before getting himself on, oh, how long ago at the top of the rapids.

Now he gathered the pieces. He trod on a heavy, rolling thing, and dropped the wood. Charlie helped gather it up. His shirt was turning to iron across his back.

He heard Wiremu moving something. He heard him open the oven door, as if that would do any good.

He heard noises he did not understand. Why was Wiremu crushing shells in his hands. What could that do?

"Paper," said Wiremu. "Siggy paper, yellow. Label from case. Paper from beans."

By feel and by foresight he had laid a fire with paper and dry twigs. But that was no use without some of the fire to set it feeding on itself.

Then Wiremu struck a match. It was as if the sun blazed in Charlie's eyes. There was something he did not understand.

The match understood perfectly well. The paper understood the flame. The flame licked at the wood and began to make it thin and black and grow a larger flame.

"They wouldn't work," said Charlie. "They've been under the sea. You can't do it."

"In the box with the beans," said Wiremu. "Box of *mati*. I brought it. Koroua has nothing to do down there but watch fire. We have the worst work to do, so I bring *mati*."

"We did not need to carry fire," said Charlie.

"Pakeha," said Wiremu. "We need them one day. This is the first day. We cannot go back to yesterday's fire. We cannot go back at all."

By firelight they saw what other wood there was. By fire heat they broke open a tin of beans and heated it, not very hot but slightly scorched.

"Fish tomorrow," said Wiremu.

Charlie's beans swam about in the water he had drunk and sent up belches. Mama would have acted severe. He leaned against the oven and it was warm on his back.

In the morning Wiremu had gone ashore, jumping over the side before Charlie had his eyes open. Charlie did not feel like jumping anywhere, stiff and sore, and scraped down one arm. His feet found the deck wasn't where they thought it was, and he walked about clumsily. He put wood on the small smoulder of fire.

Wiremu came back with a straight bough, and examining the knife carefully. It was showing signs of wear and needed a day's polishing and sharpening, to put the silvery gleam on its edge again.

Charlie pulled off his shirt and hung it in a patch of sunshine to dry. Wiremu climbed the rope into the ship and laughed at him.

"You get flowers all over your back," he said, pointing to the oven door, where there was a moulded decoration. He ran his finger over Charlie's back, where the pattern was indented. Charlie could feel it with his own hands, like a stranger's face.

They half filled last night's bean tin with water, boiled it up into soup, and drank it. There was nothing else at the moment. Then they began the day's work with the bough.

Some of it was hand-work too, dragging sand from under the ship, levering with the bough, moving the dead weight inch by inch down into the water again.

Rain came down. They went up and made the fire large enough to withstand it, and returned to the hopeless work. In the end they need not have striven at all, because the rain brought more water down the river and lifted the ship off. At one moment they pushed in vain, and in the next, while they rested, the ship was escaping on its own.

Wiremu was up the rope at once, falling on top of Charlie, because the rope was no longer fixed aboard. They had thought of using it to pull with, and not tied it again.

Charlie humped Wiremu up, threw the rope after him, and climbed aboard.

The ship, lazily reclining on its side, went sluggishly down the current.

It hit a rock after three hundred yards, and the bowsprit sagged. It touched another, and the remains of the rudder fell away. In the cabin the treasure sat quite still, its weight holding the vessel at the best angle.

Fishing time was a slow business, and there was no bait until they caught something, so Charlie thought it was silly to try. But Wiremu knew what he could do, and caught a fly that dropped from a tree.

"If we don't get a fish we eat the *weta*," he said. "But you catch your own."

One small fish liked the *weta*. A larger fish liked some of the small one. A second larger fish liked another part, and at last they had three fish.

"We could stop and pick some big leaves," said Charlie.

"You do that," said Wiremu. "I don't know how."

Charlie looked. He saw where they were really

placed. They were on a shipwrecked boat that ought not to float at all, in a river that was not fit to sail on, and the ship was running away with them, because all they had to steer or sail with was one bough from a beech tree. There was no anchor, there was no sail, there was nothing to steer with.

"It isn't going to work," said Charlie. "It hasn't worked all the time. If we get back to Jade Bay look what has happened to it. It isn't how it should be, and no one will ever find Liss, and no one will ever find us. The Koroua will die and no one will ever know anyone."

"That's it," said Wiremu. "I'm glad I brought the *mati*." He rattled the box. Charlie could tell from the sandpaper sides that only two matches had been struck from it. One had been on one side, the second on the other. Wiremu had used the second, but who had used the first. Charlie thought it was Papa, and that if somehow Jade Bay woke up out of its dream of ruin, then Papa would be there, Mama would find Liss, and Liss would tell them where her brother was. The Koroua, of course, could not tell strangers anything. Waving of arms is not exact language.

Wiremu scaled a fish and slit it open. He laid the guts aside for bait tomorrow. In the oven was a rusted grid shelf. He shook rust off it, laid it on the fire, and began to grill fish.

Charlie wrapped the bean tin in rope and dipped it over the side, bringing it up full of sweet river water.

"On ships they keep watch," he told Wiremu.

"*Ae*," said Wiremu, agreeing with him.

They let the river keep watch, and went to sleep.

"We shall have to stop," said Wiremu. "There is no firewood left after tonight."

The river carried its strange lumber along under the night sky, Wiremu dreaming of the land before pakehas, Charlie spending the night in school, listening to Miss MacDonald, feeling happy to be where nothing happened; where Siggy coming in and gazing at Miss MacDonald was the day's excitement, a big change.

17

Some days you are glad to be alive, Charlie thought, when you look back and think what might have happened two days ago. And even if I have scratches all over me, bruises everywhere, and aches in muscles, and feel hungry.

He was waking up, with a feeling of having got somewhere, of having stopped, the journey over.

Somebody was fussing about, he decided. He found it was Wiremu, who thought the journey was over, who knew they had stopped, and who was frustrated by it. He was looking over the side of the ship, trying to find out why it had stopped moving, though the water appeared deep, and was running fast.

Charlie gradually remembered the rest of life. He had a clear longing for breakfast at home, interrupted always by someone coming to the store for an urgently needed article.

They were usually people going out in boats, fishing, or perhaps round to another place altogether. Papa always served them, and Mama kept an eye on the teapot.

Charlie longed for a cup of tea.

Wiremu used one of the forbidden Maori words.

"We have to stop," he said, when he heard Charlie moving about.

"We did," said Charlie. They had.

"We are in the middle of the river," said Wiremu. "So what's stopping us? I want to be near the bank to collect dry wood, and this is hopeless, because we can't go any further."

They were both in very cold water before long, Wiremu diving down to see what the problem was. He came up spluttering, his hair almost blue with wetness.

"The ship has touched the sand," he said. "We want more water, or a big pull out. The sand comes near the top of the water. Also part of the ship has fallen out and is holding it still. I do not know what we can do."

The ship was in a wide part of river, between low cliffs, but with plenty of room for a flat bank on either side. It was a flat bank in the middle of the river that held them back now.

"It is a lazy river," said Wiremu. "It is not working."

Charlie thought of walking on beside the water. He could not draw what he thought, but it was something like a plan of the river curving round to the right and bringing them in two days to Jade Bay, where Liss was, where the Koroua waited.

"We have to work instead," said Wiremu.

"I don't want to go back there," said Charlie, thinking of the empty town. "I want to go to the real Jade Bay."

"It's one of those dreams," said Wiremu. "It's what you wanted to see. But I didn't see what I wanted to see."

"It can't be a long walk," said Charlie.

"We can tell the divers where the ship is," said Wiremu. "They could come back up and find it."

Charlie did not know what he wanted to do, or what he could do. He was sure that if he wanted the treasure he would have to tell no one about it. The divers hadn't found it, and he had, so they could not claim it. But if there is nowhere to claim it at, no one to claim it from, then it is not treasure. There were no shops in The Knuckle, and only the shell of one in Jade Bay.

There was a tin of pork and beans much closer to hand. It began to fill their minds until it had to be chopped open and shared out, half the tin each, shared before anyone tasted, using the empty tin for one share. Wiremu shared it out, then Charlie chose which to have.

The fire was so unhappy that they waded ashore, pushing the *moki*, and loaded firewood up. There was a great deal of fallen wood, which had to be cut out with the knife, broken by hand if possible, and brought back to the ship. The fire did not sleep. They felt it wanted something to eat, and fed it.

The water in the river dropped lower. Their morning's work was wasted, they knew. The ship settled a little further over to one side, and something inside it groaned unhappily and creaked stealthily.

It was impossible to do anything useful to set it free. It had set as hard as a mountain in its present position. In the falling river new rocks began to show. A spider tied the ship to one of them with a thread and built its web out and across, and waited in it.

"Gone fishing," said Charlie, waiting for it to drop a hooked line.

Charlie watched Wiremu. Shall I be able to tell, he wondered, when he decides to walk out instead of waiting for this ship to start again? If he goes would I dare stay, to look after the treasure? What could I eat?

Wiremu was hungry too. They made smoky soup on the fire, and sat drinking it from the tins, cutting their lips on the sharp edges left by the knife. There are worse edges on a tin opened with the proper opener, Charlie thought, getting a splinter in his tongue. He thought of Liss cutting herself, of the tin gradually eating her, closing its lid over her, going back into the wooden box; of the tin being opened and having her smile in it, and, oh, such lots of hair. But she smelt so delicious.

He woke up when Wiremu touched his arm, and was back in the empty wilderness.

"Someone is coming to the *kaipuke*," said Wiremu.

Charlie sniffed. There was a smell of food. He looked quickly to see that Wiremu was not cooking a private and unshared meal. He was not. All the same, there was a smell of food coming from somewhere. There was cooking.

There was a noise outside the ship. It is only Korouas walking about, Charlie thought. We know how to deal with them. He went on to think that they had been lucky with theirs, and that a Koroua here might not be friendly, and might be hungry,

155

already had a fire going, and was cooking on it. Not him or Wiremu, but was it Liss?

"Captain Cooker," said Wiremu quietly, knowing the smell of pig when it came through the air. Captain Cook had brought the pigs, so the Maoris called them after him.

From a long way off there was a new sound. Wiremu sat up on hearing it. Charlie knew what it was. Maoris were singing a song, out in the forest, singing and getting ready to eat. The noise came through the trees, more than one person singing, more than one exploding out the deep notes that came blundering through the trees like boulders from the mountain, able to knock their way through whole forests.

"Do not speak," said Wiremu. "I do not know who they are."

"They are from Jade Bay," said Charlie. "Who else will they be?"

"We do not come into the *Ringaringa*," said Wiremu, using the Maori name for Hand, or Knuckle. "They are from far away. Perhaps we have a war with them. Pakehas do not know, but we have wars among our people, and with the pakehas."

Charlie was sure he had no war with anyone. But possibly more things than Jade Bay had changed since he left. The Maori wars were over, finished at Waitangi long since. Miss MacDonald had told him. Wiremu had not been listening, that was all.

"We all belong to the Queen," he said.

The singers stopped their song. The person cooking the Captain Cooker did something to make the smell more distinct. The soft evening air carried it strong as steam aboard the ship. There were other things cooking too.

"*Kai*," said Charlie. "Food."

"They could be from our pa," said Wiremu. "I do not know the voices."

"Perhaps they are looking for you," said Charlie.

But before they had time to think about that there was a noise very close, and men were looking at the ship.

"They do not know what it is," Wiremu whispered. "They cannot think."

"We shall not tell them of the treasure," said Charlie.

"We shall keep quiet altogether," said Wiremu.

The visitors were not about to leave the ship unexplored. There was a heave and a grunt, and a splash as someone left the water and came up the side, with a lift from his friends.

"*He aha?*" he said, coming over the side and standing all to one side on the deck. "*Nga tane iti*," he told the people outside the ship.

"*Tokohai ratou?*" asked someone outside.

"*Rua*," said Wiremu.

"Two," said Charlie. "Have you come for us?"

Another man came up. They looked round to make sure that two boys were the only crew. They were amazed to find Charlie was a pakeha. The talk went so fast that he could not understand it at all. The mixture he spoke with Wiremu was quite different, and a lot of Wiremu's words were English ones said in a Maori way.

In the end there was laughter, and a great deal of telling each other that Wiremu was a fool and had been too much with the pakeha. He and Charlie were lifted down from the ship and led off into the forest, and told to look out for the Koroua. It was nonsense, they said, that they had got away from the Koroua.

"It is all right," said Wiremu to Charlie, in the middle of this teasing. "These are from Poneke, and they have come for the green stone to take home. It is understood, they are allowed to come for it. It happened long before the pakeha came here."

A Maori wanted to know what that meant. Wiremu told him.

"It is all right, he says," said Wiremu. "When they are over here they do not eat pakeha."

There was laughter about that, and a little sadness, Charlie thought, on the lines that no one would miss a lost boy anyway, so why waste the chance?

There was a big meal in the twilight, right into the darkness. By daylight the next day men were still taking early breakfast, or perhaps another helping of last night. When everyone was finished the bones went into the fire, and that was that for the day.

Wiremu had a long talk then. Some sort of discussion went on for half an hour. Wiremu explained later on what it had been about, mostly seeing whether he had any relatives who were their relatives too, because they were all related somewhere. Wiremu did not know of people far enough back, and had to give up. What he wanted was something simpler, which was some help with the ship off the sandbank, and some cold Captain

Cooker and roots. He gave something in exchange, and Charlie knew about that before the explanation.

The men looked at the problem. One of them put a great shoulder against the planking and shoved. The boat rocked obediently. Wiremu tried the same, to show that nothing at all happened for him.

The same man went under the water and looked at the sand bar. "*Ae*," he said. They could do something.

Before they did it they wanted to know the value of what Wiremu had offered. He showed them. He had bargained away half their box of matches. The men were delighted when sparks and choking smell came from the match head and flame crawled on the stick. Wiremu blew that match out, and a man tried to light it again.

Of course, they had no difficulty with fire, and made it when they needed it. They thought the matches were more interesting as fireworks, and that the bargain was good.

Charlie thought later that they had lifted the ship all in one movement, but never thought it could be true. But by pushing and heaving and grunting together they set it free from the sand and it settled down into deeper water.

They wanted to come aboard and do something to make it lie level, but understood when Wiremu pointed out the holes that were out of the water when it floated to one side.

They ran the ship along the water until it was in deep water, and then laughed at the silliness of the idea. "*Kuare*," they shouted, and that the ship would *totohu* before long, sink.

"We shall be there before that," said Wiremu. "We have had all luck all the way."

"If we had not been washed on shore we would not have the treasure," said Charlie, thinking that now they would certainly be with the Koroua and Liss by the next day. And that some time in the future the Queen herself would send for him, so that he could show her the treasure. She would make him a Mister, although he was too young, just the same as she made famous older people into Sir.

"Come to the front and help with the steering," said Wiremu. "The river is sending rocks at us and you are dreaming."

"We are glad to be alive," said Charlie, remembering yesterday morning, when nothing wanted to go right.

Today did not want to go right, either. Wiremu spoke the truth: the river was sending rocks at them, rocks floating, jaggedly, heaving up and down, knocking pieces from each other, hurrying towards the ship to do the same to it.

18

The air over the river grew very cold. Fringes of mist hung round the water, and among trees of a dark and thin kind. Charlie could not tell how tall they were because the mist went into cloudiness overhead. He shivered, even though he was working hard to push the ship away from rocks in the water, and from the edge of the river itself. And, of course, the floating rocks had to be fended off too.

The ship did not move fast. In fact it seemed to be going more slowly, but it was very stubborn, not wanting to be guided at all. Charlie shivered, wondering whether the branch was doing any good at all, whether it wouldn't be more sensible to chop it up and make a good hot fire.

"The ship is sinking," said Wiremu. He thought about it for some time, after the Poneke Maoris said that it would *totohu*.

Charlie was trying to make him look further ahead, at what the river did in the next few yards, where they would be in the next few minutes, but they had their hands full with a nasty beaky black rock, like a tin-opener, ready to slice the lid off the boat and empty the treasure into the bed of the water.

The spiky rock took a peck at them. The ship waved its stern, and what Charlie had seen took it over. There was water that looked like boiling soapsuds on washday, with rising and falling backs of hard dark clothes showing here and there. Spray was being shot into the air, some of it staying as mist, the rest lashing down like rain to make the swirling foam more angry.

If it would boil over an edge then it would, thought Charlie. There go Papa's work trousers, coming up for air, and on that side Mama is boiling a raincoat. And here we are trying to stir them with a matchstick cut from some little forest tree.

Wiremu looked ahead, and did not know what rock to stay away from. The ship began to grate over what was there, carried along in the boiling confusion, being lifted and dropped, turned and shaken, spattered and flooded by water in the river, in the air, falling from the cloud overhead. The tree bough hooked itself on an iron upright and cowered close to the ship's side.

Some of the water splashes showering the deck were lumps of ice, striking hard, smashing, skidding across the slope, and catching in the gutter inside the rail, or spinning off the edge like a roaring stone, humming hard and slapping into the water.

The ship turned right round. Charlie and Wiremu were helpless at the front of it, and here in most danger. The hull was being twisted and warped, and the planks were making a noisy protest. Charlie felt the deck moving inside itself, one

162

plank pulled forward, another back, so that his toes experienced one thing, his heel another. Wiremu looked at his own feet once.

Most of the time they looked at what was round them. In one direction was where they had come from, looking peaceful and sunny, with smooth water, the trees green and gentle, the rocks they had tried to avoid harmless, a place where there had never been a storm.

In another there was a surging river going away from them, towards the light again, angry at first, bruised with darkness, heaving with temper, but without rocks.

The third direction showed something they had never heard of and could not give a name to. There was a valley, as wide as a river at the bottom, and high as any ridge they had crossed with the Koroua. It was full, stacked with snow that blew over their own river, and solid with a green and blue ice. The ice was melting, and rills of the melt cascaded in falls from ledge to ledge, or directly from the top to the bottom. Among these pretty tumblings of water blocks of the green ice dropped into the water, and then did something alarming.

Charlie did not know much about ice. No one at Jade Bay had any, and there was hardly a frost there. The only piece he had known came from a refrigerated boat, and was left on the wharf, cloudy white, not clear, not even very clean. Charlie had waited until the boat went with its load of lamb carcases, and then gone for it. By then it had melted. There was a puddle, a wisp of lambswool, and nothing more.

He did not even think this was the same stuff.

He did not think this place was part of the world. He thought it was the mouth of some other existence coming up from the ground, being drilled through the rock. The pieces coming away were like the fragments from the bit of the carpentry brace Papa used for setting up shelves. An iron thing would come from the ground, Charlie thought, and another Papa would blow through the hole to make it clear. Last time all the dust had gone into Charlie's eye, because he was still looking through. Papa had thought him such a fool.

He did not know that ice floated, that large rocks of it could hurtle towards him on the surface, then leap into the rough water and frisk about, rubbing their sharp corners against his ship, his treasure; and that he would not think about the ship, or the treasure, or even Wiremu, but wonder about being crushed and frozen when he was not ready for it, when he did not know whether he would get home or not, when he could not think at all, really.

Then he was sure the drill was coming through, because the whole face of what he could see, the breaking icy snout of the glacier, shivered and fell away in an ice-quake. The ice came down as hard as rock, and heaped up a new huge wave in the narrow valley, and pushed it out into the river where the ship was floundering.

The great amount of water, pouring into the river from one side, made the air cold and the trees dark, and caused the roughness and the whirlpool. There was a dreadful jangling of crashing ice, like metal on metal, and flashes like sparks or lightning.

"What is it?" Charlie asked, shouting, wanting to hear a voice, hoping that Wiremu could tell him, and say he knew about it but had forgotten, that this place, that noise, cold, tumult, were perfectly ordinary, nothing to worry about; that they were harmless and would go away before morning; that Mama could be beside him and calm him.

Wiremu had known nothing about this place. "It is the South Pole," he said. "No one has been here to mark it on the map."

Then they know about it, thought Charlie. Half the worry of such a place is wondering whether it is really there, whether it is sensible to mention it, whether it would embarrass someone in the way that Liss would make a remark quite loudly about something you pretend not to notice.

I have noticed this, Charlie told himself. It is as real, as loud, as awful, as swallowing hot tea, like a sword inside that can't be pulled out. But that time Mama had just looked at him and left him to his burning. This time she was not here, and that was dreadful, until he realized that she would have been even more frightened than he was.

And all the time the spider that had built a bridge from boat to rock was quietly stitching the rail of the boat to the swinging corner of the bowsprit.

Wiremu had the knife in his hand, like a wild thing, and was chopping at the ship, cutting, cutting, at the place where the bowsprit sprang from the hull.

It was not wildness. He had seen that the long spar would strike the cliff at the turn of the whirlpool, and that the ship might leave the circuit if nothing hindered it.

165

A moment later Charlie was pulling him back, understanding the other half of what could happen, that the bowsprit, which is only a mast pointing forward and is thick and heavy, might be pushed back or to one side.

They crouched to one side. The bowsprit touched, quite delicately, choosing the right moment, and then began to push at the rock roughly. The rock took no notice. All it did was open its mouth and bite, or perhaps the bowsprit pushed into a crack or hole and was held there.

The ship lifted, its weight coming on the bowsprit, and the weight of the river behind it took it forward.

The bowsprit was torn away like a tooth that has been knocked out. Charlie knew about that, falling down the school steps when he first went at six and was too excited to look where he was going. He had got up to find a gap in his mouth, a tearing feeling running down from his nose, and Mama dabbing at him until he stopped being sorry for himself. The tooth had a long root, red and ugly. A long time later the tooth beside it had come out, with no root at all, a proper child's tooth, Mama had said.

Now the same accident happened to the ship. A bowsprit is not added after the ship is built, but put in deep as the rest of the ship is made. Its roots are deep. When it came out the deck burst open, the bow itself was gashed and hurt, the bowsprit, like the tusk of a sea beast, came out complete, stuck in the rock, spat out by the boat, and was left behind.

The ship felt the pain. It rocked and shook, and

166

there were screams of wood inside. Then it was out of the whirlpool, taken by a new and fast section of river, dark and fast as blood, and hurried away, water breaking over the fore-end of it and creeping within like mice in a roof.

That's that, said the spider to itself, and went on making a ball of silk from the hank it had already out, starting again in its busily efficient way.

"Nobody told us about a place that," said Charlie.

"They don't know," said Wiremu. "But that must be the green stone they get. They come from Poneke for it."

"I'm scared," said Charlie.

They sat on the deck, wet through, getting warmer by the minute, until after half an hour the sun was burning them and raising steam from the ship. Charlie could smell the tar between the planks.

Before nightfall another river joined theirs, bringing a clear blue stripe of different water with it on the left-hand side. The muddy water they had come down was not allowed to mix with the pure blue, and kept to its right-hand side.

"Maori," said Wiremu, nodding to the brown. "Pakeha," nodding to the blue. "One river but two streams."

A bird came dipping and bobbing in the water, now in one colour, now in the other, white and bright and quick.

"Liss," said Charlie.

A strange fish came up and looked at them, gaping and showing teeth. It seemed to walk lumpily on the water, before flopping down loudly out of sight.

"Koroua," said Wiremu. "This river is too big to go to Jade Bay. This river just goes to the sea. I don't think this boat will take us to Poneke. I think it will *totohu*."

"We will jump off," said Charlie.

"Where?" said Wiremu. "*Kai hea*?"

Charlie thought about that. At any rate there was no sign of the sea yet. And he thought the Koroua was right about coming to Jade Bay before the sea. Korouas knew such things, surely. It was only Charlie who did not know what had happened to Jade Bay itself, who could not tell whether it would come right the next time.

He thought of all the people waiting for him, and had to go to blow the fire larger and have smoke in his eyes.

It's me, he told himself, and he knew he was right, it's me that wants to meet me at Jade Bay, at the proper Jade Bay with all the real people around.

"The smoke makes my eyes water," he told Wiremu, when he came back from looking into the river from the shattered front of the ship.

"My eyes have tears in them," said Wiremu. "I am sad because my people are lost, and their pa is not in its place, and there are things no one understands, and there is no one to tell me. We should have gone to Poneke this morning in the canoes."

Charlie had not seen any canoes. They had been at the sea on the other side, Wiremu said, and the Maoris had walked for a day to gather rock. He

168

wondered again about the big pieces floating in the water. "Perhaps I should not know that," he said. "It is not good to know what is forbidden."

They did not feel hungry until they began to eat. Then they felt dry as well, and sleepy.

"What else can we do?" said Wiremu. "We have been taken by the river, and go along with it. It has not killed us yet, so perhaps we shall live."

Charlie wondered about that. If I was going to die, he thought, I wouldn't bother to eat this bit of cold crackly Captain Cooker. I wouldn't need to. So it must come right.

The ship at twilight was moving slowly down the middle of the river, not doing anything alarming at all. Once or twice it had rubbed its lowest part on mud, and moved on again, something in the water lifting them away.

"We shall stay awake," said Wiremu. "And watch. We cannot stop it."

"I will say my prayers," said Charlie, and began to sort them out. It was too late for Wiremu, and his eyes closed as the first stars opened. The prayers came out backwards and muddled in Charlie's head, and leapt about like onions falling off a table. "I'm asleep," Charlie thought, and he was.

In the dark later on the onions still seemed to be bouncing round on the kitchen floor. But it was the floor that bounced and made Charlie's teeth chatter.

Wiremu woke too, and in starlight they saw each other's eyes.

"The fire," said Wiremu, raking in the charcoal, burning himself, turning the red side up and blowing it alive. By feel he split wands of dry wood

169

into slivers and set them to melt on the glow, until flames were born.

The ship shook continually, like Elisabeth's pram being hurried along the wharf, the flat-topped tree trunks humping the wheels up, the cavities between dropping them, Elisabeth gurgling as her head shook.

When they had made something to come back to, they went to look ahead, behind, to either side.

"It is the tide," said Wiremu. "Before we were asleep the tide came up the river and lifted us from sandbanks, and we went slowly, slowly, because the water stood still. Now the tide is running out and we are going with it, and we shall be out at sea."

"Where this ship sinks," said Charlie. But he was to be wrong. That happened almost at once. Something showed up ahead of them, right across their path, like a house. The ship went into it, because it raced and the other thing stood still, waiting for the ship. It brought it to a crushing standstill, burying them in splintered wood.

19

The splintered wood was dry. It crunched under the weight of the ship. It split loudly, it snapped like rifle shots. It heaped itself overhead, it sneaked along the deck and stabbed at legs.

Quite carefully and deliberately, it prepared kindling and put it on the new and hungry fire in the grate. It sent along some larger pieces first to clear the way, to make the shabby chimney tumble overboard, to get right under the remaining roof of the cabin, to bang impatiently at the oven door.

Wiremu was rather ridiculous, Charlie thought, to want to rescue his matches from the oven. There was enough fire here for a week.

The ship itself, stopped so sharply by something it could not get through or bounce off, had to continue to go. Heavy things must go on moving until the energy has worn off. This heavy thing could not push through, could not go round, could not go over. It could only go down. When it did water gurgled in at the broken bow, clambered up the steeply dipped deck and into the cabin, and the ship went down faster and faster.

There was room under the water for it. The river was deep and pulling it along and down. The front dived and the stern continued forward, bringing fire to the middle of the thing it had run into.

It took Charlie some time to work out what was happening. They had not hit another ship, or merely a tree. The wood that had skirmished round his knees and tried to pin his hand against a post was not raw tree wood. It was sawn wood, made into something.

"We've got somewhere," he told Wiremu.

Wiremu was busy climbing about the strange framework that the ship was still destroying, seeing by firelight what there was, not knowing how to understand it, but getting out of its way. There were huge timbers, roughly squared, that the ship had lifted from their places, and was now dropping back noisily into the wrong ones.

Wiremu settled for the knife, and saving his skin. Charlie thought of the tins, and of some Captain Cooker and could not find either. He smelt the Captain Cooker being roasted again, and that was all. He did a walking upside-down backwards somersault through a tangle of deadly wood, found himself on one of the massive beams, and went along it although it was moving.

He got himself out of the fire and on to dry land, and waited for Wiremu. Wiremu did not come. Only the flames rose and rose on the tidal wind, burning what there was to burn. Below it the ship writhed and bubbled, and some of its tar began to spurt thick yellow flame and blazing trickles of bubbles.

The wood burst with reports like maroons. Sparks and smoke lofted into the air, lit underneath with red fire, coiling up and up.

Somewhere in the mountains, Charlie wondered, are they seeing this? He had the midnight thought that this was the very fire, the very light they had seen; that what they found in Jade Bay was not the site at all.

They were burning something that blocked the river. No, it was burning itself. It should not have been there. Beyond it he saw something move. Wiremu was on the other bank, had got across somehow, and was running up and down looking for Charlie.

Charlie knew what they had done, what they had set on fire. He only knew of one, but there must be others; and this must be one of the others.

He sat down to watch it happening in the warm night. After it there would be nothing, he knew. The treasure was now lost for ever, the ship was sunk, Wiremu was the wrong side of the water, and everybody was left alone. At this moment he knew the Koroua would be tired of Liss and would walk back alone to his lake, taking the sheep, taking the beans and the tin-opener, taking back the doll, and longing for the knife.

Liss would wander in the forests and become a Koroua herself, in a tangle of fair hair.

Some of this was a dream. He woke with a hot face to a dying fire and a morning beginning.

There was a very angry and large Maori farmer hitting his shoulder and speaking very quick and loud, not able to manage any pakeha words, hardly able to manage his own. Charlie blinked at him for some time and gathered his thought.

When he had done that and looked around,

seeing what he saw, he laughed. That made the Maori farmer angrier again, but it could not be helped. On the other side of the river, at the far end of the burnt-out bridge, a pakeha farmer was shouting at Wiremu, and Wiremu was not understanding his words.

Charlie was glad the pakeha was there, because that stopped the Maori hitting him, or throwing him into the river, or even doing a quick barbecue and breakfast with him. Wiremu was glad the Maori was there, so that the pakeha farmer did not kick him into the river. No one would want to discuss that sort of thing with a Maori of that size.

Wiremu was shouting too, but to Charlie. He was taking no notice of a pakeha farmer. "We burn down the bridge," he yelled. "Not our fault. The bridge get in the way. We didn't put the *arawhata* there."

Charlie was getting a lot of *arawhata*, or bridge, from his own Maori. There was much signalling across the scorched timbers, and some useless kickings at them and shakings of heads. Wiremu was shouting insults to the Maori, but Charlie was not so adventurous.

No one but Charlie and Wiremu knew what had happened, and there was no way of explaining it to pakeha or Maori. Of course you come down the river in a ship, but of course you also don't if it means smashing our *arawhata*. So speech got them nowhere.

The pakeha shouted across to Charlie to stay where he was, because the Maori was going to town to get things sorted out and paid for. However, Wiremu was not staying alone with an angry

174

pakeha, so he proceeded along his bank, still shouting at the Maori, taking no notice of the pakeha. Charlie went along with the Maori, and the pakeha farmer had to follow.

There was a bend in the river. And Charlie began to wonder why they had not met the farmers before, because ahead of them was the little wooden spire of the church, and across the road from it the walls of the school.

Which was all very well, but impossible to understand, because no one could build the school so fast, straighten the church, restore the houses . . .

Charlie began to feel faint with trying to understand. Church and school, old or new, broken or whole, spun round in his mind until he could not see what was there.

"Tenei matou," said his Maori. "Here we are. Now we shall see to you."

Charlie was unable to walk. His head was filled with dizziness, and his legs were weak. He did not know where he was at all, and they refused to work unless they knew for certain. He began to sink to the ground.

The big Maori picked him up and carried him into Jade Bay. Then, not surprisingly, put him down in front of a house with a verandah all round it, a window with goods behind it, and the name C Snelling painted neatly on a new board over the steps.

The Maori shouted. It was early in the day, but Papa came out of the door, frowned at the Maori for shouting when he should have come to the door in a civilized way, and waited to see what happened.

The Maori paddled Charlie across the road with a hand on his back, operating a puppet. Papa looked down sternly, and then looked up.

"No," he said.

"Papa," said Charlie.

Papa had to look again before knowing it was Charlie. He blew his nose while he thought about it. He held on to the post of the verandah.

"Mama," he called. Charlie wondered why he was using another voice.

At that moment the pakeha farmer came hurrying up. "Had to get a ferry across the river," he said. "You know what these boys did?" But he stopped suddenly, unable to say anything. It had not occurred to him that the pakeha boy might be Charlie, until he saw the storekeeper pick him up and carry him into the house.

There was no Elisabeth in the house. Only Mama by the fire, very thin and white, and breakfast for two, only Papa's plate used at all, a slow sad kettle dropping steam by the fire, and the curtains not pulled quite back.

"Liss?" asked Mama, holding him hard, but only half as much as if both were there. "Liss?"

"She is here," said Charlie, saying it and finding it impossible. "We brought her here with the Koroua."

"Tell the truth, son," said Papa. "If you can't tell the truth you might as well go away again."

"Liss," said Mama. "Where is Liss?"

The town doctor came in a dirty coat. He had been seeing to a calf. He looked at Charlie, peered

176

round for the other one, Liss, and said nothing but, "Sleep, food, and the truth, for you my lad."

"But there was a Koroua," said Charlie.

"Drink this," said the doctor, tipping out some black drops into a cup of water.

Later on Papa was still being grim about Charlie's return. Even Charlie could not make sense of the story he told. Elisabeth was already here, with the Koroua. People looked at him, and then looked away.

"Do not say it again," said Papa. "And now we shall look at the bridge you burnt down. This is no way to come home. Why did you not stay away if this is all you can say or do?"

"There is treasure," said Charlie. "I know there is treasure. I have seen the boxes."

Papa did not say anything while they walked back to the bridge. People were coming from either side and not being pleased at all. They had all paid for the bridge, and now the storekeeper's son had burnt it down, along with a rascally Maori, and no one would find him, and the Maoris had no money, so who was to pay?

Charlie had another go at explaining, but Papa told him to stop talking that half-and-half lingo and stick to English; he had had to do it himself, and Charlie must too.

One of the divers came up just behind them. He was able to talk to Charlie without blaming him for anything.

"Not seen you since that low tide," he said. "My, the wave came in something terrible, gave the town the go-by, and smashed up the coast down along. You wouldn't think they had the

177

strength in on the Mainland to get an earthquake that size."

Charlie did not know what he was talking about, just heaping words together. Perhaps divers are not very clever, he thought. But everyone is cleverer than me. Where is Wiremu?

Papa had to agree that something more than fire had happened at the bridge. It was not fire that had lifted the main timbers out of their places, and it certainly was not two boys, or even ten boys.

"Old ship in there," said the diver. He could tell even through the newly-risen tide. "Nearly on her beam ends, just a boat really, about forty feet long, you can't see much. Lost her rudder, lost her mast."

"And the bowsprit," said Charlie.

"Reckon," said the diver. "She's too steep in to have kept that. Well, what boat is it?"

"It's yours," said Charlie. "It's the *Alexander*. Papa, we shall be rich."

There was silence when he had said that.

"I'm sorry he's such a stupid boy," said Papa.

"If he's been away," said the diver, "he wouldn't know. No, son, we found the *Alexander*, and got everything out of her. It was a paid job for the government, and they took every piece of gold, every piece of silver, and all the copper coins. It's called specie. They got the lot, and we got the fee. They knew exactly what was there, even the dates on the coins."

"I'm sorry," said Papa. "I'll do what I can to put matters right. I don't understand his games, and I don't approve of them. All I know is that he has come back without his little sister."

178

"We brought her back," said Charlie. He said it a second time, and then shouted it. "We brought her back and she stayed with the Koroua. We brought her right back into Jade Bay, all in the ruins."

Papa's hand had been flying out to hit Charlie on the head. But the hand stopped. There was a big silence. Everybody turned and looked at Charlie. Only the diver did not, turning away to look at the wreck in the river.

"Someone will have to get it up," he said, hoping for the job.

No one took any notice of him. Charlie was the centre of attention now, being looked at in silence, being looked at with interest.

What have I done now? he wondered. What have I said? I didn't mean it. What else can be wrong?

20

An hour later the diver had a job, not of lifting the ship from the bottom of the river under the bridge, but of getting his own salvage boat ready for a journey.

Since the long stare and silence beside the bridge Charlie had been ignored, because people were now too busy. One woman he knew had asked how he was, and Miss MacDonald had smiled at him on her way to school. That was better than being treated with scorn. Charlie could feel the blow he nearly got from Papa, up by the bridge.

But still he was not certain what was now happening. Mama said nothing to him, but she had become more lively, a touch of colour was in her face, and she had looked in the mirror and smiled. She gave Charlie breakfast, not very much of it, and not what he had ever liked.

But that did not matter: any food at home tasted like real food, even warm bread and milk, with sugar, in a basin. The milk was from a cow and had no taste. Charlie was used to the richer bite of sheep's milk; and bread he had forgotten.

"We had silver spoons," he said.

Mama took the basin away. "We'll see," she

180

said, "when . . ." She would not say her hope out loud, but at least she now thought Charlie's story might have truth in it. She was heating water in the wash-house, believing he should be washed yet again.

Somebody brought Wiremu down from the Maori pa. He did not want to come down, because he had been blamed for all sorts of things, even for causing the flood, which had come into the town and done some damage, but not much.

He sat on the verandah of the store and would not come inside. An older Maori, not the farmer who had captured Charlie, but one who was probably Wiremu's grandfather, said he had now grown very wild, and that his stories ought not to be listened to. But really the grandfather did not want to think of the Koroua, because the thought alarmed him.

"No good," said Wiremu to Charlie. "Where are they all going?"

"They didn't tell me," said Charlie. "In a boat. I don't know what I said, but they stopped getting ready to hit me."

"What are you going to do?" asked Wiremu.

"Go to school, I expect," said Charlie. "Or get bathed. I don't know. Why did we come back?"

Men were bringing their guns to the store. Charlie thought there must be a hunt. They were buying ammunition. Papa was putting on an outdoor coat and getting down his gun, looking through it, filling his pockets with bullets.

The school bell rang. No one sent Charlie to school. He said nothing. After a time he went in

181

to see what was happening, to ask whether he could come too.

Siggy had left the telegraph office for the day. He was in the store with his own gun. Charlie was glad that nothing important was happening. Though news of earthquakes was welcome, it had been followed by unusual events.

"We're going to settle with whatever took your sister," said Siggy, snapping his gun into its proper shape now he had looked through it. "Settle and proper."

"The Koroua?" said Charlie. "He didn't take her."

"We know where it is," said Siggy. "And it'll know where we are. It's a dangerous wild beast"

"But," said Charlie, "he isn't. He . . ," Charlie tried to think of a good argument. "He uses plates to eat from."

"So does a dog," said Siggy. "You shoot dogs."

"The Koroua is a pakeha," said Wiremu. "We came here to find him, but it's the wrong river."

"We know that," said Siggy.

"Only two very stupid boys do not know that," said Papa. "We shall see about the truth of your story, and there will be no more Koroua. So Wiremu, go back to the pa, and Charlie, stay inside the house. One way and another you have caused enough trouble, and when we come back you may have more."

"He is your child," said Siggy. "The other one is nobody, and it is from him that trouble comes."

"We shall know the truth tonight," said Papa.

The diver came to the store then. He wanted more rope, not being certain about moorings, he said. And that's a lot of guns, he suggested after a time.

"We've always known about monsters in The Knuckle," said Siggy. "I'll be sending a tale of the end of them over to Auckland before the day is out, you see."

"But you are wrong," said Charlie. "You are quite wrong. If he is dead it is because he has died already. He was very old and could not walk unless we helped him."

"Stop your nonsense, Charlie," said Papa.

"That's right, Carl," said Siggy.

"Well," said the diver, "I'm not sure about guns on my boat. And if this boy met a Koroua, then he was not frightened by it, so how's that for a monster? I reckon you should find out a bit more before shooting it, or him, or whatever it is. After all, if you find your little girl happy and unharmed, then what's all this talk of wild animals? As far as I can tell she'll be better off out there with him, than back here among the bloodthirsty savages of Jade Bay."

Siggy looked at the floor. Papa turned and straightened some things on a shelf. Mama opened the door at the back of the shop to call Charlie through for a soak in soapy water.

"Yeah," said Siggy after a while. "We don't know, right. But we are ready to know."

"You will frighten him," said Charlie. "He didn't frighten us."

"Charlie," said Mama. "Come along."

"You listen to him," said the diver. "You believed him about one thing, why not try him on another. I think he's telling the truth. And these

183

two are the only ones who know the wild man, so they should come with us. If he's as wild as you make out then he'll need friends, and if it's true and they know him, then you must hear his side too."

Papa nodded. Mama called for Charlie again. Papa waved her away. "They had better come," he said. "I do not know what we shall find, but they will be able to help."

"If they were there," said Siggy. "If it is not all fancy, and if we don't discover worse."

"They're living on pork and beans," said Charlie. "Someone left a case of tins there, and an opener, and some telegraph paper, beside a big bonfire."

"That's where they went," said Papa. "I didn't think they had all been eaten. I thought, they have been hidden and not paid for, fallen off a horse."

The diver's boat went down the tide. Charlie was hunkered in the bottom of it, out of the way of the sail that swung from side to side, always when it seemed settled in its place and going comfortably.

The guns were lodged under the bow, where there was a cupboard. The diver, Mr Johansen, steered and gave orders about the sails. Waves came to look at the boat, pushing it from side to side, now and then peering inside and throwing spare water over Charlie.

After a time his back grew cold in a strange way. He had to kneel up and look over the side. The bread and milk slid softly into the waves, and a slap of water washed his face.

"Can't be helped," said Mr Johansen. "But it's

over for you now, and you don't feel like it any more."

"I do," said Charlie. But at the same time he didn't if he kept his mind off it. Mr Johansen gave him and Wiremu a rope end to tidy up and squabble about.

Papa and Siggy were the only men Mr Johansen had allowed in the boat. He had turned out four already in when he came back with his coil of new cord. "We shall need room to bring back whoever we find," he said.

"Alive or . . ." Siggy was beginning, thinking only of the Koroua, and then remembering that they were mostly looking for Elisabeth and wanted her alive.

"There were lots of beans," said Charlie. Two hours later he was not able to think of beans.

Siggy was charting the way for the diver, who had never had to think of what was on the coast, only of its shipwrecks out to sea. "That big headland," he was saying, "like a cat's paw stretched out. Part of The Knuckle. We want to be beyond that."

"Another hour and a half," said Mr Johansen, buttoning his coat against a sprayey shower of rain. "Wind just right for going each way slowly. We'll go out to sea for a bit. "You got any more breakfast ready, Charlie?"

The slow swells further out to sea were more comfortable, and Charlie began to enjoy the swing and movement. The sun came out and the sail dried. Wiremu curled up and went to sleep. Charlie leaned on the side and felt very sleepy himself.

185

The choppy pitching of the boat at the mouth of a river woke him again, close to land.

"This is it," said Siggy. "I haven't been by sea since, you know, the last time. But at mid tide like this we can go in anywhere in a small boat like this. We shan't notice the shallows."

"There is a big rock in the middle further up," said Charlie. "The Koroua caught a big fish there."

"I know the place," said Siggy. "My brother and I would fish there because the big ones gathered there for meetings some time in the day and the tide."

They came to the shore. From here there was nothing to see of any town at all. Charlie wondered whether they had come to the right place, whether everything had been muddled through with nobody listening to what anyone else said.

He saw a building on the bank, and knew he had seen it before, that it was where the Koroua had fished by the rock.

"There it is," said Siggy, meaning the rock.

The sail rattled down. "Now what are we doing?" said Mr Johansen. "Are we acting without thought?"

Papa and Siggy thought about things.

"I'm going to look for my daughter," said Papa. "I think it needs a gun."

"It doesn't," said Charlie, contradicting Papa, a thing he had not done before without terrible consequences.

"He's right," said Mr Johansen. "The boy is right. If what he says is true, let him go first. If what he says is not true, then we don't want him back, do we?"

186

"Something like that," said Siggy. "We'll let him go first and follow close behind, ready to set things right if we have to."

"We know where she is," said Charlie. "And him."

"Right," said Wiremu. "She's playing storekeeper in the store, and he's living in the church beside the whalebones."

"It is possible?" asked Mr Johansen, looking at Papa.

"Yes," said Papa. "They have been here. That's true. Now for the rest."

He got out of the boat first, took the guns from Siggy, and Siggy followed. Charlie and Wiremu got out on their own. Mr Johansen came ashore and tied a mooring rope to a tree.

A moment or two later there was a smell of wood smoke. "Must still be burning," said Papa, thinking of the big fire the men had made a week or two earlier, looking along the coast for three children. He was not willing to admit anything good about the Koroua.

The fire was near the church. "See," said Charlie.

"Yeah," said Siggy. "We see."

Charlie wondered again whether he was really here, in this broken and worn version of Jade Bay. No one had explained anything to him. But now ahead of him was the store of C Snelling, as leaning and dropped as before, when he had seen a fresh new store exactly the same, without trees growing through it, without falling signs or steps, earlier this very same day.

Then, before he saw quite what it was, a small

furry thing, brown in colour, came squealing out of the doorway and running towards him, shouting his name.

"Liss," said Charlie. A great blurring began in his eyes and he could not say another word. But Elisabeth had turned away from him and was running to Papa, shouting his name, stumbling on her skirt, scrambling up again, and babbling words no one could understand.

Papa let her climb up him and cling and cling, which he did not often permit. Today was different. Instead of standing he sat down, flat on the ground, and the gun fell from his hand. He actually gave Elisabeth a kiss on her forehead, something he only did once a year on her birthday. Her tears were running down her face, and his tears running down his.

Elisabeth took no notice of Siggy, She ran to Charlie and hugged him, and butted her head happily against Wiremu.

Charlie went towards the church, where the fire was. The Koroua was standing there, listening, wary. But he knew Charlie, and smiled. Charlie took him by the hand and led him across the road.

Siggy turned and looked, fidgeting with his gun, rattling an imaginary telegraph button on his way. Siggy dropped the gun, quite carelessly, and put his hand to his head. Then he moaned, fell right down where he stood and turned on his back.

21

They had a full load on the journey home. Mr Johansen sat and shook his head slowly all the way back. There was Papa, severe again but still holding Elisabeth, who slept and woke and babbled whichever she was doing.

There was Siggy, still feeling pale, and very ashamed of it, holding the Koroua's hand and now and then bursting into tears himself.

Wiremu and Charlie were there, but together at one side. The other was laden with a large stone, the name on the underside, but read by everyone, Ludwig Webber.

There were no sheep. There had been long discussions about them, but they had been cut loose from their ropes, to run free. Instead they had followed the Koroua down to the river, not wanting to lose him. They hardly understood about being free.

There were three tins of pork and beans. The Koroua had insisted on bringing them. Elisabeth made a face at them, because she had seen enough.

"There is no need," Siggy had said. "Erich, there is no need. I have forgotten my German." The Koroua had forgotten his too, and had not

189

expected anyone to speak English. He had rather thought that New Zealand was a German colony, because that was where Jade Bay began, pronounced in a different way.

There were the bundles that the Koroua carried everywhere. There was a fuss with him about carrying fire on board; and then he remembered he had been shipwrecked.

There was the doll called Treasure.

Mama took Elisabeth away at once, when she met the boat. She shied away from the Koroua, but Elisabeth held his hand, and took a wooden comb from him, before going off. She came out from the bath Charlie should have had cleaner, but not quite clean yet, and in her night gown.

There was a meeting in the school the next day. The diver had been down to the ship up the river when the tide was low, and had hauled out nine boxes from the twisted cabin. They were full of water, very heavy, and were draining a dark fluid out in the road. Mr Johansen had also found another thing, but did not show it to anyone yet.

The boxes had not yet been opened. Charlie knew they were treasure, and that was that.

"After an earthquake," said Miss MacDonald, when she had the whole town sitting at the desks, and most of the children on the floor at the front, "and the earth has moved, there is often a tidal wave that travels across the sea to other countries. Before it gets there, and why we don't know, there is often a very low tide. Charlie and Wiremu and Elisabeth did not know this, and went out on the low tide. And then what, Charlie?"

190

"We found a ship on a rock, right out of the water," said Charlie. "It was called the A L something on the bell, but the bell fell down and got lost. Then the tide came in."

"We had a telegraph message that morning," said Siggy. "About a giant wave. It had been to Gisborne, Napier, and all over. We tried to get everyone back by ringing the school bell and the church bell, and firing maroons."

"In the end," said Miss MacDonald, "we had everyone but Charlie and Elisabeth. And Wiremu, from the pa."

Elisabeth took her thumb out for a moment. It steamed.

"So what happened next, Charlie?" asked Siggy. He was still holding the Koroua's hand. The Koroua was dressed in his own clothes. He had sewn them up in sheepskins a very long time ago, and he had grown in some ways since them, so his shirt and jacket were very tight and extremely old fashioned, and the trousers were tight and too long for his misshapen legs.

"The tide came back," said Charlie. "I don't know where we went, but we ended up in a lake."

"*Tote* in the water kill all the fish," said Wiremu.

"The Koroua found us," said Charlie.

"My brother is Erich Webber," said Siggy, stroking the Koroua's hand.

"Koroua," said the Koroua.

"He looked after us," said Elisabeth. "He is my best friend. He made me a doll."

"Then he tried to get us back," said Charlie. "We helped him, because he couldn't walk."

191

"He did his best," said Siggy. "Didn't you, Erich?"

But the Koroua was still thinking and hearing in German.

"We followed the light and we got to Jade Bay," said Charlie. "It's just like here, only broken down. We did not understand. There was our store."

"It was a long time ago," said Papa. "Siggy knows best."

"Jade Bay was founded at another place," said Siggy. "But the place would flood every year, and we had to move it. But we liked it, and we had the original town plan, so we made the new one the same as the old one. I call that sense. We brought the school with us, and we're in it now. The foundations are still at the old place. We meant to go back for the church, but it was easier to build a new one from the same plans."

"And my father, Carl," said Papa, "which is my name, and Charlie's, but he's forgotten that. We all came from Germany. Well, he had the store before me, and the last thing to come round by sea was the town's little ship, the *Albrecht Dürer*, full of store things."

"Treasure," said Charlie, because by now he knew where the story was going.

"But it never got here." said Papa. It had on board my uncle Ruprecht, a Maori sailor, and Erich Webber, Siggy's brother. It was wrecked, and no one came ashore alive."

"But here is Erich," said Siggy. "Fifty-one years later, and very well. He could not find his way out of The Knuckle, and at first he did not mind because the visiting Maoris were kind to him, but never managed to take him on their canoe and land him anywhere. They gave him fire. Then, when he was trying to come out alone he slipped and fell from some great height, and both his legs were broken. He nearly died, but in some way he managed to move about, and he has managed ever since, quite unable to walk out alone. He lit fires, but everyone knew he was drowned, and that the wild men lived in The Knuckle. No one looked for him. You know, he was fourteen years of age at that time, and I was four. Now he is sixty-five, and has only spoken to Maoris from the Mainland since then. No wonder he has forgotten all his good German words, like me."

"We were going to shoot him," said Papa. "We did not think."

"*I* was going to shoot him," said Siggy. "My own brother. We brought back our father's gravestone, to stand in the churchyard here."

"Also your great uncle, Charlie," said Papa.

"Of course," said Elisabeth. "The best one. He thought I was his little sister."

"Ja," said the Koroua.

"She went back to Jade Bay in Germany," said Siggy. "Where we came from. I have sent a telegraph message."

"And then?" said Miss MacDonald, getting back to the story of what happened in The Knuckle.

"We found the town had gone wrong," said Charlie. "So we went back for the boat to come down the river with it."

"Sail to Poneke," said Wiremu.

"I thought it was more earthquake," said Charlie. "I thought," and something began to crawl round his nose, perhaps a *weta* or other insect. "I thought," and still his nose tickled, and a tear ran down outside it and several more inside, because of what he had thought. "I thought you were all dead."

"You didn't tell me," said Wiremu. "I did not want to hear."

Mama got up and came to Charlie, sitting beside him in a desk, putting her arms round him, holding him tight, which she never did now. There were tears and bubbles and slothers from Charlie down the firm soft front of her dress, but she did not mind. Elisabeth looked on patiently, making allowances for feeble things like brothers. Charlie used a handkerchief, and his sleeve, and felt extremely happy. He pushed Mama out of his desk seat, and got ready to continue his story.

"We crashed into the bridge," he said. "And burnt it down. We did not know. The boat sank, and I thought it was treasure."

"We don't know what it was," said Papa. "I don't know how you come by these ideas."

"But the Koroua," said Charlie, "knew the skull that was in it. He cried over it and buried it." He was unashamed of his own tears, remembering the Koroua's.

Siggy talked to the Koroua. The Koroua said, quite clearly, "Ruprecht, ja," and nodded his head a lot, smiling black teeth.

"That was my uncle Ruprecht Snelling," said Papa. "It must be."

"And just to check it out," said Mr Johansen, coming forward with a cloth bundle in his hand,

194

"I went down in the ship this afternoon and brought this out."

He uncovered the bundle, and there was a great gleaming thing under it, bright as the sun, and ringing as it was touched, the black name on it clear now, *Albrecht Dürer*.

"The ship's bell," said Mr Johansen. "A little ship to have a bell at all, and a big bell for it too."

"That is simple," said Papa. "The German settlers came here on a big ship, the *Albrecht Dürer*, from Hamburg, in 1840. They bought the bell when that ship was broken up at Wellington. It was the town bell, and for that voyage, the last one between settlements, uncle Ruprecht fixed it to our little ship."

"Now we shall look at the treasure," said Mr Johansen. "There will be nothing there." He had brought levers and hammers with him, and went through the boxes one by one, wrenching them open.

He was right. Papa was right, for box after box. One after the other held nothing of any value, only more boxes that had held tea, or still held the black berries of coffee, or the rusted out machine to roast and grind them. Another was full of books turned to pulp, a third had rotting cloth, black and stinking.

The fifth, which had been heavier than most, did not hold treasure, exactly, but had been carefully packed with china plates and cups, still in tissue wrappings, and hardly broken at all, because outside the tissue was sawdust that had set nearly solid in the water.

"Those are mine," said Papa. "they are worth money. You are right, Charlie. But bringing them has cost the town a bridge. I think we shall send them over the sea again to Wellington or Auckland, and see what they are worth there. They are after all from the best factory in Germany."

Another box held a sewing machine, and one for stitching boots. The boots were still there, not quite finished, and named for Carl Snelling, Papa's Papa, who had never worn them. Siggy's father had made boots then. Siggy made them still while he waited for telegraph messages.

The last but one was filled with smelly mud. Papa said it was the remains of all the store spices, and picked out some seeds he knew, still with the smell, but turning to wet dust between his fingers.

The last box held sheets and sheets of leather. "But there is nothing wrong with these," said Siggy. "They can be washed in clean water, and will make boots again. This is of value, Carl."

And, right at the bottom, there was another box full of silver articles. "I forgot to mention them," said Papa. "They were lost too, of course. They are the ancient silver from our home village in Germany, and they belong to the whole community and to the church. Charlie, you have been right after all. I will say," he added after a thought, "I will say that someone should give him, and Wiremu, three cheers."

"We will," said Siggy. "He has brought more treasure than we could think of having. Hip hip," and while they shouted he hugged Erich.

The Koroua cheered too, and Elisabeth went to

cheer him, by herself. She was not going to cheer for Charlie.

But Papa did, and Mama, and quite loud, Miss MacDonald.

Later on, in the excitement, and in the same schoolroom, when they went back to continue their talking, Siggy was bold enough to speak very seriously to Miss MacDonald. She blushed very greatly, then took his hand, drawing him to the front; and he drew Erich after him.

"There is something personal I have to say," said Miss MacDonald, "to avoid rumour. Mr Sigismund Webber has asked me to become his wife, and I have accepted."

"You will have them both to look after," said Papa. "You know that."

"I will look after the Koroua," said Elisabeth. "He looked after me."

"Liss," said the Koroua. "Ich bin Erich."

"Ja," said Elisabeth.

Siggy's telegraph messages for the rest of the week were all returned as unreadable, and for the next week as unbelievable, and the week after that he and Miss MacDonald went off man and wife ("Christabel," he whispered to Charlie, "is her name") to Wellington.

But that night, after the schoolroom, the Maoris from the pa came down to collect Wiremu and Charlie, and anyone else who wanted to come to a *hangi*, food roasted in a pit, a meal lasting all night, for eating, and all the next day for finishing off and recovering. The Koroua had hiccups from the fizzy Maori beer.

197

"The boy is such a fool," said Papa affectionately, during the third Captain Cooker, and carried him round the pa and into the meeting house where the men smoked and told stories nearly as wild as the one about the Koroua.

Join the RED FOX Reader's Club

The Red Fox Readers' Club is for readers of all ages. All you have to do is ask your local bookseller or librarian for a Red Fox Reader's Club card. As an official Red Fox Reader you will qualify for your own Red Fox Reader's Clubpack - full of exciting surprises! If you have any difficulty obtaining a Red Fox Readers' Club card please write to: Random House Children's Books Marketing Department, 20 Vauxhall Bridge Road, London SW1V 2SA.

Other great reads from **Red Fox**

Further Red Fox titles that you might enjoy reading are listed on the following pages. They are available in bookshops or they can be ordered directly from us.

If you would like to order books, please send this form and the money due to:

ARROW BOOKS, BOOKSERVICE BY POST, PO BOX 29, DOUGLAS, ISLE OF MAN, BRITISH ISLES. Please enclose a cheque or postal order made out to Arrow Books Ltd for the amount due, plus 75p per book for postage and packing to a maximum of £7.50, both for orders within the UK. For customers outside the UK, please allow £1.00 per book.

NAME_____

ADDRESS_____

_____

Please print clearly.

Whilst every effort is made to keep prices low, it is sometimes necessary to increase cover prices at short notice. If you are ordering books by post, to save delay it is advisable to phone to confirm the correct price. The number to ring is THE SALES DEPARTMENT 071 (if outside London) 973 9700.

Other great reads from **Red Fox**

Spinechilling stories to read at night

THE CONJUROR'S GAME Catherine Fisher
Alick has unwittingly set something unworldly afoot in Halcombe Great Wood.
ISBN 0 09 985960 2   £2.50

RAVENSGILL William Mayne
What is the dark secret that has held two families apart for so many years?
ISBN 0 09 975270 0   £2.99

EARTHFASTS William Mayne
The bizarre chain of events begins when David and Keith see someone march out of the ground . . .
ISBN 0 09 977600 6   £2.99

A LEGACY OF GHOSTS Colin Dann
Two boys go searching for old Mackie's hoard and find something else . . .
ISBN 0 09 986540 8   £2.99

TUNNEL TERROR
The Channel Tunnel is under threat and only Tom can save it . . .
ISBN 0 09 989030 5   £2.99

Other great reads from **Red Fox**

Share the magic of The Magician's House by William Corlett

There is magic in the air from the first moment the three Constant children, William, Mary and Alice arrive at their uncle's house in the Golden Valley. But it's when they meet the Magician, William Tyler, and hear of the Great Task he has for them that the adventures really begin.

THE STEPS UP THE CHIMNEY

Evil threatens Golden House in its hour of need – and the Magician's animals come to the children's aid – but travelling with a fox brings its own dangers.

ISBN 0 09 985370 1   £2.99

THE DOOR IN THE TREE

William, Mary and Alice find a cruel and vicious sport threatening the peace of Golden Valley on their return to this magical place.

ISBN 0 09 997390 1   £2.99

THE TUNNEL BEHIND THE WATERFALL

Evil creatures mass against the children as they attempt to master time travel.

ISBN 0 09 997910 1   £2.99

Coming in June 1993

THE BRIDGE IN THE CLOUDS

With the Magician seriously ill, it's up to the three children to complete the Great Task alone.

ISBN 0 09 918301 9   £2.99